'How dare you pry into my life?'

'It is private—I won't be discussed like some tacky pin-up just to satisfy your idle curiosity!'

Lizzi held her breath as Ross's almost silent footsteps took him to the door, then he paused.

'Thank you for the toast and coffee. It's a long time since a beautiful woman's cooked my breakfast—and, for the record, my curiosity wasn't idle. I had every intention of acting on it.'

He left her rooted to the spot, speechless.

Dear Reader

We're travelling the world this month! Angela Devine bases her story in Sydney, and, as well as being a marvellous romance, it makes a good case for donating blood. Frances Crowne takes us to Germany and troubled teenagers, while Lilian Darcy explores an unusual area of Canada. Closer to home, there is another excellent story from Caroline Anderson—you will adore Ross! Enjoy. . .

The Editor

Caroline Anderson's nursing career was brought to an abrupt halt by a back injury, but her interest in medical things led her to work first as a medical secretary, and then, after completing her teacher training, as a lecturer in medical office practice to trainee medical secretaries. In addition to writing, she also runs her own business from her home in rural Suffolk, where she lives with her husband, two daughters, mother and dog.

Recent titles by the same author:

SAVING DR GREGORY
PRACTICE MAKES PERFECT

MORE THAN TIME

BY

CAROLINE ANDERSON

MILLS & BOON LIMITED
ETON HOUSE   18–24 PARADISE ROAD
RICHMOND   SURREY   TW9 1SR

For Sarah and Hannah, who make it
all worthwhile.

*First published in Great Britain 1992
by Mills & Boon Limited*

© Caroline Anderson 1992

*Australian copyright 1992
Philippine copyright 1992
This edition 1992*

ISBN 0 263 77745 6

*Set in 10 on 12 pt Linotron Times
03-9206-49184*

*Typeset in Great Britain by Centracet, Cambridge
Made and printed in Great Britain*

CHAPTER ONE

IT WAS a typical April Fool's Day joke, Lizzi thought disgustedly—and a sick joke at that.

Having caused havoc overnight, the unpredicted snow had now turned to slush, and a steady gentle rain was washing away the last traces. The white mantle that had fallen silently over the countryside on Sunday afternoon had had its fun. Now, on Monday morning, everyone was making their way to work, the mayhem forgotten.

As she turned into the hospital car park, Lizzi wondered what she would find on her ward as a result of the weather's little games. No doubt orthopaedics would have come off worst, but there were bound to have been a fair smattering of internal injuries resulting from the inevitable car pile-ups. With a little frown she wondered how they would find room.

Her mind on her work, Lizzi turned sharply into a space and then gasped in disbelief as her obedient little car ignored her explicit directions and sailed gracefully into the side of the vehicle on her right.

As it ground to a halt, Lizzi sat stunned for a second and then wriggled out of the passenger side and walked reluctantly round to inspect the damage.

'Ouch!' she winced. Her front wing was scraped and the light cluster was cracked, but that wasn't what was

5

worrying her. It was what it had scraped itself *on* that made her heart miss a beat.

She walked round to the rear of the car and read the badges. 'Daimler Double-Six. Damn. Wouldn't you know?' A further inspection revealed that under the layers of road dirt the car was the same dark forest green as her own, but, unlike hers, it was a mess inside and out, with crisp packets and apple cores scattered all over the back seat on the otherwise immaculate cream leather. Whoever owned it didn't deserve to, she thought with a sniff, looking proudly at her well-kept Metro. She had bought it in August, and it was still in showroom condition—or it had been until a few minutes ago!

With a heavy sigh, she slid back into her car, worked her way across behind the wheel, and reversed carefully out of the space, slotting herself in again with rather more accuracy.

As she stepped out, her feet shot out from under her and she slithered awkwardly into a pile of slush. She muttered something distinctly unladylike under her breath.

Someone had obviously been here over the weekend and had recently cleared the snow off his or her vehicle, leaving it in a pile—the pile she had just happened to hit as she drove in.

Picking herself up, she brushed off her coat and, ignoring a twinge in her shoulder, reached inside the car for a notepad.

Then she looked for the staff permit on the windscreen.

Nothing.

Well, would you believe it? she thought. Seizing her pen, she wrote her telephone number, instructed the owner of the car to contact her that evening, and added a cryptic note to the effect that if the car had been in the visitors' car park where it rightly belonged the accident wouldn't have happened.

Shaking the crumbs out of an old sandwich bag, she slipped the note into it and tucked it under the Daimler's windscreen wiper before locking her car and headed for the entrance.

She was too late now for a cup of coffee in the staff canteen, so she headed straight for her ward.

As she passed the entrance to the ward, she noticed almost absently that there were several new faces, and an obvious reshuffle of patients around the ward. She frowned. She liked her patients to get used to one station, keeping them there if possible at least for the duration of their convalescence, if not from immediately post-op. Too much change just confused them and slowed down their recovery, and that wasn't to anyone's advantage. She knew that the night sister agreed with her, so there must have been something fairly drastic going on to necessitate the changes.

She went into the staff cloakroom and hung up her coat, then rolled up her sleeves, straightening the white cuffs automatically. Glancing in the mirror, she frowned at the light mist of raindrops which clung to her blonde hair. A few fair strands had escaped and curled in damp tendrils round her neck, softening the severity of the look. She tucked them firmly back into the bun she wore at the nape of her neck, and pinned her lace cap on absently, her thoughts still on the patient reshuffle.

Her wide violet eyes troubled, her soft mouth set into a firm line, she strode briskly into the ward kitchen and came to an abrupt halt.

It seemed to be full of people, although on closer inspection there were only two. Still, they filled it. A tall man in theatre greens waved a coffee-pot at her and smiled wearily.

'Hi. Coffee, Lizzi?'

'Please, Oliver. I didn't have time. What's happened to you? You look as if you've been run over by a truck!'

'God, you do wonders for a man's ego, Sister!'

Lizzi snorted. 'I'm not here to do wonders for your ego, Mr Henderson. You have a wife for that.'

'Mmm. I'll have to remind her—if I ever get the time!' He waved the coffee at the other man. 'Ross?'

Her eyes swivelled towards the stranger. He was tall, taller even than Oliver, and well made, neither gangly nor heavy. His coffee-cup seemed tiny in the long, strong fingers. His forearms were dusted with dark hair, and in the V of his green theatre tunic she could see crisp black curls edging the hollow of his throat. His lean hips were propped against the worktop, his feet, still in anti-static boots, crossed at the ankle.

Weary though he undoubtedly was, he exuded a sort of natural energy, a healthy coiled strength that hinted at youth and vigour, but that was misleading. His most startling feature was the mass of soft, thick silver hair which looked casually tousled—as if a woman had just run her hands through it, Lizzi mused, surprised at the untypical and highly personal direction of her thoughts. As she watched, he thrust it back off his face with those lean, hard fingers, rumpling it even further.

Then he lifted his head and their eyes met, and Lizzi blinked. Warm, gentle grey-green eyes, eyes that seemed to see straight through her façade. She suddenly felt totally exposed—and very vulnerable.

'Sorry, you two haven't met, have you? Lizzi, this is Ross Hamilton, our new consultant. Ross, Lizzi Lovejoy, our own personal whirlwind.'

'Sister Lovejoy.' Ross extended a hand, and Lizzi found her own engulfed in its warmth and strength.

'Welcome to the madhouse, Mr Hamilton.'

One side of his mouth lifted in a wry, lop-sided grin that made him look years younger. She realised with a shock that he was, in fact, much younger than she had at first supposed. It was his silver hair that aged him, that and tiredness.

And he was, she saw, quite exhausted. There were bags under his eyes, and shadows, and the lines bracketing his mouth were harshly etched, as if he had been overworking for weeks—or even years.

As she took all this in, he turned to Oliver and refused another cup of coffee.

'I want to go to ITU and see a couple of patients, then I really ought to try and get respectable before my outpatients clinic.'

He ran his hand over his jaw, rasping against the stubble and, coincidentally and unexpectedly, Lizzi's nerve-endings.

'OK. I'll catch up with you at lunch,' Oliver replied.

'Uh-huh.' His voice was soft, deep and husky with a Scots burr that was strangely attractive.

He crossed the tiny kitchen in a stride, and Lizzi watched, transfixed, as he reached her. Tall as she was, he was so close that she had to tip her head back to meet his eyes.

A smile flickered around his full, firm lips. 'I'm sorry to run away, but I've been in Theatre all night. I'll come and see you later.'

Lizzi felt a rush of confusion. Why should he want to see her? She felt threatened, strangely excited. Close up she could see the rough stubble on his jaw, and he looked utterly disreputable and totally fascinating. A surge of adrenalin brought a flush to her cheeks and a pulse to life in her throat. Her lips moved soundlessly.

His brows twitched together, and he seemed to have difficulty dragging his eyes away from her lips. Unconsciously, the tip of her tongue came out to moisten them, and his eyes flicked up and tangled with hers for an endless moment.

'Yes, later,' she managed, almost normally.

'Good.' Still he stood there, as if he was waiting for something. 'Excuse me,' he said, and then the smile which had been waiting sprang to life on his lips and touched his eyes with subtle humour. His big, strong hands came up and cupped her slender shoulders, and he moved her gently out of his way before brushing past.

Lizzi realised, belatedly, that she had been standing like a fool in the doorway, blocking his exit. She watched him walk away, his stride confident, unhurried, yet covering the ground at a good speed. So that was him, she thought, the much talked about James Kinross McKenzie Hamilton, BSc, MB, BCh, FRCS. . .

Oliver was watching her speculatively. 'Coffee?'

'Thank you,' she murmured, and dragged her mind back into a professional gear. Ross was out of sight now.

She turned back to Oliver. 'I take it you've been busy?'

'Hell on wheels. That snow really screwed things up. I've been here since five o'clock yesterday afternoon, and Ross rang in at six to find out if we needed help.'

Lizzi took the coffee from him and stirred it thoughtfully. 'That was good of him.'

Oliver nodded. 'He's a damn fine surgeon. We were lucky to get him. He's been going flat out all night, and he's only just finished moving in to his new house. I gather he'd been to Scotland over the weekend and just got back down yesterday afternoon before the snow started. He said he'd been running in his new car rather faster than was advisable!'

Lizzi frowned. She didn't want to be reminded about cars just then. 'So, what's new on the ward?'

They gravitated back to her office, deep in conversation, and Lizzi found the night sister and the nurses on the early shift gathered for report.

'Morning, all,' she said cheerfully, and quickly pulled up a chair. 'Sorry to keep you waiting; Mr Henderson was just filling me in on the new admissions.'

The night sister, Jean Hobbs, flicked open the Kardex, and went systematically through the patients.

The additional information on the three new ones caught Lizzi's attention.

The first, Roger Widlake, was a man in his forties who had suffered severe internal injuries, including a ruptured spleen, punctured lung and ruptured liver following an RTA. 'No doubt he'll drive more carefully in future if he lives long enough,' Jean Hobbs commented.

'Why isn't he in ITU?' Lizzi asked, horrified.

'No room,' Oliver put in. 'They're run off their feet. He's in a side-ward—Hamilton operated on him. He'll be back down later; he wants to talk to you about his care.'

So that was why he was coming back. Lizzi felt a little surge of disappointment. 'How stable is he?'

The night sister shrugged. 'Difficult to say. He's only been down from Recovery for two hours. We'll have to watch him like a hawk.'

Lizzi nodded. She would put Sarah, her best staff nurse, on to special him for the morning at least.

The next patient was a woman with similar but less severe problems. Jennifer Adams had sustained a ruptured bowel and a messy abdominal tear when her steering-wheel had snapped and penetrated her abdominal wall.

She was, Lizzi thought, extremely lucky to have got off as lightly as she had.

Oliver joined in again. 'There was a minor abrasion on her left ureter, and her left ovary was also slightly bruised. Apart from that she's fine, and came through surgery very well. She's had two units of whole blood but she's on saline now. Her worst problem will be scarring, I suspect. I've done my best, but she'll probably need plastic surgery later.'

Lizzi nodded. She had seen these sorts of injuries before.

The third patient to catch her attention was a young man of twenty, Michael Holden, who had been thrown clear of his car and then run over by another vehicle, causing a whole range of internal injuries.

'He should definitely be in ITU!' Lizzi protested, mentally assigning herself the task of specialling him.

'He will be,' the sister replied. 'They'll take him as soon as they can clear a bed. They've got a head-injuries patient they're hoping to transfer to Addenbrookes, and a spinal injuries case for Stoke Mandeville as soon as he's stable enough. That should clear two beds. I would think they'll take him then. Of course, if the bloody fool had been wearing a seatbelt——' Jean Hobbs looked up and smiled. 'That's it, then. Over to you!' She flipped the Kardex shut, stood up and stretched. 'You're welcome, let me tell you!'

Lizzi smiled grimly. The week had really got off to a flying start, she thought with disgust.

She sent Sarah Godwin off to relieve the night nurse with Roger Widlake, put her other staff nurse Lucy Hallett in charge of the ward and headed off with Oliver to see Jennifer Adams and Michael Holden.

Jennifer was feeling very sorry for herself and Oliver wrote her up for more powerful pain relief before leaving her and taking Lizzi into Michael Holden's room.

His breathing was very light and harsh, and his face

was pale and clammy—the bits that weren't bruised and cut, at least.

'How is he?' Oliver asked the staff nurse sitting at the head of the bed.

'His respiration's very irregular, and he seems to be in pain. His pupils are still uneven and unresponsive, and he doesn't react when you talk to him, but he's very restless. We had to tie his hands down because he kept going for the drip.'

Oliver nodded and studied the chart for a moment, then the heart monitor. 'It'll be a miracle if he makes it. He's a mess. I don't think I've ever seen such massive internal injuries except in a post mortem.'

'I'm surprised he hasn't broken anything apart from a few ribs,' Lizzi commented.

'He probably has. The radiographer's coming up to X-ray him again. There was so much blood mass obscuring the plates it was difficult to see, but his pelvis is a definite candidate. The orthopods will come and see him later if he hangs on long enough. I reckon the head of his left femur cracked the acetabulum as he landed, but we'll see. He could also have a slight skull fracture.' He glanced at his watch and gave a short, tired sigh. 'I must get on. Will you be all right?'

Lizzi gave him a wry grin. 'I'll do my best. What about Roger Widlake?'

'Ross will be down to talk to you about him before long, I expect. See you later.'

Lizzi scanned the charts, smiled at the nurse and told her she could go. 'I'll special him,' she said. 'Could you ask Lucy Hallett to come and see me in a minute?'

But it was Ross and not Lucy who opened the door

a few minutes later. He walked over to Lizzi and stood close to her as he studied the chart.

'How's he doing?'

Lizzi shrugged. 'Not well.'

Ross shook his head. 'I doubt if he'll make it. He's so badly shocked, and he was under the anaesthetic for hours. Oliver and I were working on him together.'

Lifting up the edge of the bedclothes, Ross frowned at the drainage bag from the catheter.

'His kidney's been bleeding a bit.'

'Kidney? Just one?'

'We had to remove the left one. It was shot to bits.'

They watched dismally as a steady trickle of blood ran into the bag.

'Damn.'

'Will you have to open him up again?'

Ross shrugged. 'Maybe.' He opened up the drip a little so that the whole blood ran faster, and checked his blood-pressure. 'Pressure's OK. I think we'll just watch him closely. It may stop on its own. The last thing he needs is another anaesthetic. He's got so much alcohol in his system that he really can't take it. His system is depressed enough.'

'He was drunk?'

'As a skunk. The police are waiting to talk to him.'

As the old familiar rage swept over her, Lizzi lost all compassion. 'Why the hell was he driving?'

'Good question. He caused the accident, apparently. Ploughed into Jennifer Adams—it's her husband in ITU with the head injuries, by the way—and then spun off and caught Roger Widlake and his wife broadside. She's fortunately only slightly injured.'

'Bastard,' Lizzi whispered. 'It would serve him right if he died!'

Ross blinked. 'That's a little harsh, isn't it?'

'It's no more than he deserves!' Lizzi said bitterly.

Just then there was a dramatic drop in blood-pressure, and the heart monitor registered a flat trace.

'Here we go again,' Ross said with a sigh, and rolled the man carefully on to his back, tipped back his head and breathed into his mouth while Lizzi automatically slid a board under his chest, then, locating his sternum, he crossed his hands and pumped steadily.

'Get an airway in, Lizzi.'

Lizzi hit the alarm button, ripped open a Brook's airway and inserted it carefully into the man's mouth, forcing her professional side to take over from the unprecedented surge of emotion. Suddenly the room was full of people. Someone took over the air bag, attaching it to the airway and squeezing it steadily in the gaps between Ross's rhythmic cardiac massage.

'Do you want the defibrillator?' someone asked.

'No, he's gone into asystole. He's just given up—he may have a ruptured aneurism. We'll have to keep him going if we can. If it isn't that, he may pick up again.' Ross snapped out instructions which had already been anticipated by the well-trained team. The atropine, calcium and adrenalin were already drawn up, and were injected into the giving set in the patient's arm, as soon as they had been checked.

There was no response, and adrenalin injected directly into the heart was equally ineffective. The trace remained persistently, stubbornly flat.

After several more fruitless minutes, Ross straightened up with a sigh. 'There's nothing more we can do. It must be his aorta—the PM will tell us. All right, thank you everybody.'

No one was surprised. The staff filtered out of the room, and left Lizzi and Ross alone with the dead man.

'Probably just as well,' Lizzi said flatly as she removed the airway and switched off the monitor.

'Aye. Maybe.' Ross sounded gruff, and Lizzi shot him a look.

'Don't you agree?'

'Depends on your reasons for wishing him dead. If it's to spare him any further suffering, then yes. If it's just because he was young and irresponsible, I think it's a bit extreme.'

Lizzi blushed. 'I'm sorry. I didn't mean to over-react. I just—feel very strongly about drunk drivers.'

Ross straightened, and flashed her a weary grin. 'Technically I agree with you, but I'd just spent several hours of my life struggling to save the young fool, and it's hard to see it all thrown away. I like working miracles, and I don't like to be cheated! But you're right, the poor bloke's better off dead. God knows what complications he would have had if he'd lived.'

Lizzi followed him out of the room. 'What about relatives?' she asked.

'They hadn't managed to contact any by the time they brought him down this morning, I don't think.'

But they had. Lucy Hallett ducked her head out of the office door and smiled.

'I've got Mr and Mrs Holden in here. They're wondering about how Michael's getting on.'

Ross and Lizzi exchanged glances, and he nodded.

'Thanks, I'll see to it. Perhaps you'd get him presentable?' he murmured quietly to Lizzi.

Lucy frowned, and Lizzi shook her head slightly. Lucy's mouth formed an 'O', and she came soundlessly out of the room as Ross went in and closed the door firmly behind him.

'What happened?'

'He arrested—probably as a result of a traumatic aneurism. Just as well. Mr Hamilton was about to have to take him down to Theatre to sort out his kidney again, because it was still bleeding. Did his parents realise how bad he was?'

Lucy gave a hollow little laugh. 'I doubt it—I didn't know, and they were getting their information from me. I was having difficulty holding them; they were almost determined to find him.'

Lizzi went back into Michael's room and took down the drip, removed the catheter and tidied up the bed. No doubt his parents would want to see him now, and she did her best to disguise the damage. Just as she was about to leave the room, Ross appeared with Michael's parents.

She left them to it. Telling relatives was a part of her job that she liked the least, and she wasn't particularly good at it. She realised she was also feeling very angry with the dead man still, and probably wasn't the best person to deal with his relatives anyway. Maybe it was cowardly of her, but she made her escape nevertheless and went to see how Sarah was doing with Roger Widlake.

He seemed to be holding his own much better than Michael had, and Lizzi went back to her office and contacted the mortuary technician, and then rang ITU to tell them that they now only needed one bed.

Shortly afterwards she saw Ross escorting the Holdens out, and she didn't see him again until much later, by which time Roger Widlake was in ITU and her ward was her own again.

She was sitting in her office doing battle with the rota when he opened the door and popped his head round.

'Can I come in?'

'Of course.' She straightened up and pushed the paperwork away from her. 'What can I do for you?'

He grinned. 'You could offer me a coffee and we could talk about Roger Widlake, in that order. I think I'm going to fall asleep otherwise!'

'Mr Widlake's been transferred to ITU,' she told him.

'Good. Then I'll settle for the coffee!'

He dropped wearily into the chair opposite her desk and rubbed his hand over his face. He had shaved and changed into a suit, but he looked just as tired.

She smiled. 'I'll see what I can find. Have you had breakfast?'

He shook his head. 'No. I'd missed the chance by the time I'd dealt with the Holdens.'

Lizzi felt guilty. 'I'm sorry I left you to cope with that. I should have done it so you could go and rest for a while.'

He gave her a weary, lop-sided smile. 'It doesn't matter. I don't suppose you would have enjoyed it either, even though you think he got his just deserts.'

'I——' Lizzi's mouth opened and closed, and she

floundered to a halt. Was she really that vindictive? Was her judgement really so clouded that she couldn't deal with the relatives of a patient because she had tried him and found him guilty?

Ross smiled understandingly. 'Don't look so worried. I had difficulty, too. It's hard to explain that someone's golden boy is not only dead but has caused havoc on the way. It was easier than I'd thought. His father asked straight out if he had been drinking, and I think his attitude was much the same as yours, but tempered by love. He's a policeman.'

'Oh.'

'Yes, oh. Lizzi?'

'Mmm?'

'Coffee?'

'Oh. Sure. Sorry.'

She left the room and went into the kitchen, making toast and fresh coffee. She found some butter and marmalade and laid a tray, and took it back into her office.

He was asleep, his head propped on his arms, sprawled across her rota. He had taken off his jacket, and his shirt pulled and eased with the rhythmic rise and fall of his broad shoulders. The sun gleamed on the soft, thick mass of silver hair, turning it to pale gold. It looked impossibly soft. Lizzi wondered how it would feel in her fingers. She felt a strange, primitive urge to nurture and protect—but not maternally. Oh, no. There was nothing maternal in her feelings, and she drew in her breath sharply.

She hadn't felt like this for years, not since—not for

years. She put the tray down with a tiny clatter, and he stirred and sat up.

'Sorry.' His voice was gruff, sleep-roughened. He ran his fingers through his hair and her fingers ached with jealousy. The elemental urge strengthened.

Grasping the coffee-cup, Lizzi filled it and set it down in front of him, her hands trembling slightly.

'Black or white?' Damn, why did her voice sound breathless?

'Black, I think. Thank you.'

'Toast?' That was better. Her voice was her own again.

'Lovely. Do you spoil all the doctors like this, or are you just taking pity on me?'

She blushed and busied herself with her own cup. He was right. Normally she would have sent them off to the canteen rather than let them raid the ward provisions. Sometimes when they were very rushed Oliver would grab a sandwich, but waiting on them? With a tray? What was she thinking about?

She knew perfectly well what she was thinking about, and she blushed again as he caught her eye. She struggled for a neutral topic.

'Oliver told me you'd had a hectic weekend.'

He chuckled. 'Is that what you call it? I picked the boys up from school in Norfolk on Friday and took them back to their mother in Edinburgh on Saturday, then back down yesterday.'

'Your wife's in Edinburgh?' Lizzi asked, surprised— as much as anything at herself. She never, *never* asked personal questions—or answered them, come to that!

'My ex-wife. Her husband's a GP. She works part-time in the practice.'

'Oh, I'm sorry. I didn't mean to pry——'

He waved the toast dismissively. 'That's OK. It's public knowledge. What about you?'

'Me?' Her voice rose, and she made an effort to bring it down. 'What about me?'

His mouth curved appealingly. 'Are you married? Engaged? Entangled?'

She swallowed. 'I——'

The phone rang, its warble loud in the sudden silence.

'Sister Lovejoy here. Oh, hello, Bron.'

As she dealt with the details of the new admission, Lizzi was aware of Ross's eyes on her as he munched his way through the toast.

When she put the phone down, he asked the question again.

She stood up, straightening her skirt with a tug. 'Mr Hamilton, I make it a point not to discuss my personal life or anybody else's with anyone at work. I'm afraid I can't see the relevance.'

She swept out of the room, collared the young houseman and instructed him to clerk the new admission coming up from A and E.

'Acute appendix, man of twenty-four. We'll put him in Bay One.'

For the next twenty minutes or so she supervised the admission of the new patient, training a student in the preparation of the charts and the taking of the first TPR and BP readings, the notice over the bed which read 'Nil by Mouth', the urine sample to be obtained if possible and the tests to be done on it, the checking of valuables and other possessions and so on down the endless list, while the houseman obtained the relevant medical information.

She had seen Oliver come on to the ward a few minutes earlier, and so she headed back to her office to find out whose list the patient would be put on. As she approached the door quietly in her soft-soled shoes, she heard Ross's deep voice murmer a question, and then Oliver chuckled.

'Lizzi? You've got to be joking! The junior staff call her the Ice Maiden—that or Sister Killjoy.'

'She's not that bad, surely?'

Oliver laughed again. 'Save yourself the effort, Ross. You'd need a PhD in cryogenics to thaw our Lizzi. She doesn't play—not ever, not with anyone!'

Ross laughed, soft and very masculine, and murmured something else that Lizzi couldn't quite hear. She heard Oliver's reply, though, and it chilled her.

'Nobody knows. She wears a wedding-ring on a chain round her neck, but whether he's dead or gone AWOL nobody knows. She may not even have been married. It could be her grandmother's ring or something. She hasn't ever mentioned anyone, though. Forget it, Ross. If it's recreational sex you're after, you need look no further than that young scrub nurse in Theatre with us last night—given a chance she'll be all over you like a rash——'

Lizzi had had enough. She swept into the room, clicked the door shut behind her and glared at them both.

'How dare you both discuss me behind my back?

That is exactly the reason I tell no one anything! And as for your locker-room comments about recreational sex—what kind of a reputation do you think you're giving the medical profession? You're behaving like a couple of medical students! Now get out of my office so I can get some work done!'

As they stood up, looking severely chastened, Lizzi remembered the reason for her mission. 'Oliver, your wife has just admitted a patient for appendicectomy. Whose list is he going on?'

'Mine. I came up to see him. Where is he?'

She glared at Oliver, her eyes furious. 'In Bay One. Dr Haig is with him.'

'Lizzi, I'm sorry——'

'So you should be!' She slapped the case file into his hands.

With a shrug, Oliver left the room, closing the door quietly behind him.

Ross picked up his jacket and hooked it over his shoulder on one finger, running the other hand through his hair.

'Lizzi, I'm sorry, it was my fault. I shouldn't have asked him about you, but I was curious——'

'How dare you pry into my life? It is private—I won't be discussed like some tacky pin-up just to satisfy your idle curiosity!'

Lizzi realised that she was flushed, her fists clenched, her chest rising and falling rapidly as her anger got the better of her. Forcing her hands to relax, she struggled for control of her temper and met Ross's eyes challengingly. His lips firmed, and his eyes flashed angrily for a second, and then another emotion flared, just as strong but somehow more shocking, and Lizzi had to turn away.

She held her breath as his almost silent footsteps took him to the door, then he paused.

'Thank you for the toast and coffee. It's a long time since a beautiful woman's cooked my breakfast—and, for the record, my curiosity wasn't idle. I had every intention of acting on it.'

He left her rooted to the spot, speechless.

CHAPTER TWO

LIZZI had forgotten about her bump in the car park. By the time she got back to her car at the end of the day, the relentless routine of the busy surgical unit had driven everything else out of her mind. Now, though, she was reminded that there could be a nasty confrontation ahead later that night, and she sighed.

The confrontation wouldn't be improved, she realised, by the fact that the offending car had also been wheel-clamped by the ground staff. She was surprised that it was still here. She was torn between smug self-satisfaction and pity, but her urge to take the note off the windscreen was snookered by the fact that it was already missing.

Perhaps the owner had been back already and was now trying to find a porter to release the wheel-clamp? Anxious to avoid a physical battle with the seething driver, Lizzi made her escape and drove home.

The bungalow was silent, with the sort of silence that meant emptiness. Her mother was out—Lizzi remembered that it was her watercolour class that afternoon, and she always went back to her friend's house for the evening afterwards. Lizzi would be alone all evening, and in her present mood it was probably for the best.

She felt restless, disorientated and unaccountably depressed. No, not unaccountably, she thought bitterly. Michael Holden, the irresponsible young drunk driver, was largely to blame. Did Ross really believe she thought he had got his just deserts? Was she really so hard? Or just too vulnerable? It didn't matter. There was nothing she could do to change things.

Lizzi went along to her bedroom and undressed, pulling on clean jeans and a soft sweater the same colour as her eyes. As she sat at the dressing-table to brush out her hair, her eyes strayed to the photo in the silver frame propped up beside the mirror.

A young man with laughing eyes looked out at her, his carefree smile showing a row of even white teeth. One of the top ones was chipped slightly—Lizzi remembered how he had come back from a rugby match with a swollen lip and she had chided him gently while she put ice on it.

Suddenly her eyes filled and she picked up the photo and held it to her chest as the tears spilt down her cheeks.

'Why did you leave me? I'm lonely now,' she whispered. She bit her lip and fought down the sobs. 'They call me the Ice Maiden, David. But I'm not really, am I? Why can't they just leave me alone?'

She rested her cheek against the cold glass, and gradually the tears slowed and stopped.

She put the picture back, rubbing the tearstains off the glass with her sleeve as she did so, then she blew her nose, wiped her eyes and went into the kitchen to cook herself something light for supper.

There was nothing on television, and the book she picked up couldn't hold her attention. She lit the gas fire to ward off the chill, and curled up on the settee with her feet tucked under her bottom. She felt cold inside, filled with a sort of dread that she couldn't place. Was it because she was waiting for the phone call from the irate driver of the Daimler, or was it because tomorrow she had to go back and face Ross and Oliver after her fit of temper? However justified, her harsh words didn't make for a happy ward.

With a deep sigh she wriggled further down the settee, propping her chin on her hand and staring into the hissing fire. Her mother wouldn't be back for hours, and she really couldn't justify going to bed at six-thirty!

Anyway, when her mother got back she would need help to prepare for bed, so there was no point.

Suddenly Lizzi realised just how blank and empty her life was. The reason she never talked about it at work was that there genuinely was nothing to talk about. By not talking about it, she was hiding that nothingness—from herself as well as her colleagues. True, she had her mother, and she was needed in her way, but all the normal things that people of her age took for granted were missing from her life. Her time was reasonably full, but her heart was empty. No man, no social life, no children—angrily she dashed aside the tears and stood up. No point in sitting moping.

She got out the vacuum cleaner and started attacking the carpets—anything rather than allow the wallowing self-pity that had been creeping up on her.

When she turned off the vacuum cleaner she realised that the phone was ringing, and she snatched it up just as the caller hung up.

Damn. Now the waiting would start all over again.

She put the vacuum cleaner away and dropped disconsolately back on to the settee. Forcing herself to submit to discipline, she picked up her book again and made herself read four pages before she went out to the kitchen and put the kettle on.

The ringing phone held her transfixed for a second or two, and then she lifted the receiver and gave the number automatically.

'Lizzi? It's Ross Hamilton.'

'Ross!' She was startled, her surprise showing in her voice. What on earth did he want? And another, more pressing question presented itself. 'How did you get my number?'

He laughed, a low, mirthless chuckle. 'Easy. You left it on my windscreen.'

She must be mad, she thought for the thousandth time. Surely they could have found a time and a place at the hospital to discuss this? Why had she suggested that he should come here? What if her mother came home early? She would never let Lizzi forget it! Oh, God!

She stomped around, bashing cushions and straightening pictures, tidying the already immaculately tidy bungalow until the doorbell rang, almost savage in the silence.

She practically leapt out of her skin, and then had to pause and steady herself before going to the door.

She wiped her hands on her jeans and smoothed them over her hair. Why was it so unruly? And why was she so thoroughly unsettled and agitated?

When she opened the door, Ross was standing in the porch, his hands thrust into the pockets of his duffle coat, a white sweater in stark contrast to the tanned skin of his throat. He looked disturbingly male, and Lizzi panicked into overdrive.

'Come in. Ross, I'm sorry, the note was unnecessary, I wanted to take it off the windscreen but it was gone when I came out. Let me take your coat. Can I get you a drink? What would you like, tea or coffee, or something stronger? Come on through.' God preserve me, I'm babbling like an imbecile! she thought, and bit her lips.

'Lizzi.' His voice behind her was full of quiet authority, and she stopped, her head bowed, and waited for the axe to fall. 'Relax. I'm not angry with you.'

She spun round, her eyes wide with amazement. 'But your lovely car——!'

He shrugged. 'It can be mended—though how you managed to wreck all four panels on that side is a mystery to me. I'm sure you didn't do it on purpose, so we'll just hand it over to the insurance companies and let them fight it out.'

'How can you be so calm? I realised after I'd spoken to you—Oliver said something earlier—it's brand new, isn't it? You must be livid!'

He chuckled. 'I vented most of my spleen in the porters' lodge!'

'Of course—your wheelclamp!' Her hand flew to her mouth to cover the grin, but he saw it and glowered at her.

'Gloating, Lizzi?'

She moved away from him, her amusement gone. 'No, I'm sorry, I wasn't—it was just the irony—Ross, I——'

'Lizzi?' His voice was deep, gentle. He cupped her

shoulders in his hands and drew her nearer towards him. 'I was only teasing. Don't be afraid of me.'

She looked up and met his eyes, then looked away again. 'I'm not,' she said quietly. 'I'm just not used to inviting men back to my house. It threw me for a minute.'

She could feel his eyes on her, studying her thoughtfully.

'Would you rather we did this another time? Perhaps at the hospital?'

'That would be silly,' she murmured. 'Anyway, you're here now.'

'It needn't take long, then I'll go, if I'm making you uncomfortable. Is it because of this morning?'

She shook her head. 'No, not really. I'm sorry about that, too. I haven't really given you a very warm welcome to the hospital, what with one thing and another.'

He laughed. 'At least it's going to be memorable!'

She tried to smile, but failed. 'We haven't really got off to a good start, have we?'

'No. No, we haven't, and at least part of that is my fault. I shouldn't have asked Oliver——'

'Then why did you?' Her question was short, harsher than she had intended, but his reply was quiet, sincere, softly voiced.

'Because I wanted to know about you. You seem so aloof, but I know you're not. No one who can blush like you did is aloof—far less an ice maiden.'

She blushed again under his gently teasing regard, and eased out of his grip. 'I'm not available, Ross. Not for—what was it Oliver called it? Recreational sex?'

He laughed softly. 'He didn't imply that you were—or that I was seriously in the market for anything so tasteless.'

Lizzi felt unaccountably relieved. 'Was she?'

He frowned. 'Was who what?'

'The girl who was all over you like a rash—was she in the market for it?'

His face cleared, and his mouth lifted in the now familiar lop-sided smile. 'I didn't even notice, to be honest. Sorry to disappoint you.'

Her relief escalated to full-blooded optimism, and she treated him to a broad smile that lit up her face and made her eyes sparkle.

'Oh, I'm not disappointed,' she assured him.

Ross's smile widened. 'Good. How about that coffee before we sort out this paperwork?'

Lizzi's face dropped. She had forgotten why he was here, and she was carrying on like a lovesick teenager!

She led him into the kitchen and they made coffee and then, sitting at the kitchen table, exchanged information about the accident, both making all the necessary notes for the claim form.

Then when all the business was completed he pushed back his chair and stood up.

'I'll get out of your hair now.'

'Oh, you don't have to go! Have another coffee or something—I didn't even ask if you'd eaten!'

He grinned. 'I have, thank you, but if it won't offend you I'll take a rain check on the coffee. I'm dying to get to bed. Sunday morning seems a long time ago.'

Filled with remorse, Lizzi retreated into herself. 'I'm sorry,' she said quietly, 'I'd forgotten you'd had such a dreadful night. Of course you must be exhausted. I don't know what I was thinking about asking you to come here this evening.'

'I'll survive. Anyway, it was a good excuse to see where you live—another piece of the jigsaw that's Lizzi Lovejoy. I intend to unravel you, you know!'

She followed him numbly to the door. She was feeling distinctly unravelled already!

He shrugged into his duffle coat and opened the door, then he turned and dropped a light kiss on her lips just as a car swept into the drive.

He raised an eyebrow in enquiry.

'My mother,' Lizzi explained, wondering how she would ever get away with that innocent kiss—not that it had felt innocent. Her lips were still tingling from the explosion of sensation that had occurred as his lips brushed hers, and she felt rocked off her feet. She just hoped her mother hadn't seen, because she didn't feel up to the lengthy evasions that would be necessary. In fact, she rather hoped he would go, but of course he couldn't because his car was blocked in and she was stuck with him at least until her mother was over the threshold!

'I'd like to meet her,' Ross murmured.

'Good, because there's no way we can avoid it,' Lizzi muttered under her breath.

He had acute hearing, if the chuckle that came from him was to be relied on.

She glanced at him. Six foot three, and fit as a fiddle, even if he was tired.

'Come on, then,' she said, 'you can make yourself useful getting her out of the car. She's disabled.'

Ross walked with her to the car, where Lizzi performed the briefest of introductions, and Ross lifted her mother easily out into her wheelchair.

'Don't forget to think about it, Mary!' the driver called.

Lizzi's mother smiled mischievously. 'Oh, I will, dear. Good night, and thank you so much.'

They watched the car out of the drive, then Ross wheeled the chair easily to the door and over the slight step.

'Thank you, dear,' she said as the front door closed behind them again. 'Now, who did you say you were?'

'Ross Hamilton—I'm working with Lizzi at the hospital. I started today.'

'How nice. I thought I hadn't heard your name. Well, it's lovely to meet you, Dr Hamilton.'

'Mr, Mum. He's a surgeon.'

'How silly that is. Fancy going to all that trouble just to deny your qualifications!'

Ross laughed. 'I quite agree, Mrs Lovejoy.'

There was sudden silence, then Lizzi's mother looked at him quizzically. 'I'm Mary Reed, actually. Lovejoy was Lizzi's married name. It used to suit her, too.' She sighed. 'Oh, well, all water under the bridge. Stop glaring at me, darling. Why are we all congregating in the hall?'

'Ross was just leaving. He had a busy night in Theatre.'

'What a pity. Still, it's lovely to meet you, Ross. I hope we'll be seeing you again?'

'I hope so too, Mrs Reed,' Ross said with his lopsided smile.

'It's so nice that you and Lizzi have made friends so soon——'

'This isn't a social call, Mum,' Lizzi cut in, her embarrassment running at full strength. 'I hit his car this morning in the car park—we were just sorting out the insurance details.'

'Oh, dear! What a shame—is it that very nice car on the drive?'

'Yes—and it's extremely new,' Lizzi commented drily. 'In fact, I couldn't have targeted a worse thing to hit.'

He chuckled. 'Let's say your daughter's car has unerring good taste, Mrs Reed.' Lizzi opened the door, and he bade Mrs Reed goodnight and followed her squirming daughter out.

'Well, Mrs Lovejoy,' Ross murmured, 'another piece in the puzzle. Will you tell me, or do I have to guess?'

'I'm a widow,' she said quietly.

'And your husband was killed by a drunk driver.'

She gasped. 'How did you know?'

His smile was full of compassion. 'I didn't, but it doesn't take a great deal of intuition to guess. Was it long ago?'

'Seven years.'

'That's when I got divorced. Sometimes it seems like yesterday, and sometimes it seems forever. I expect you feel the same.'

'You can hardly compare the two,' she said stiffly.

'Why?'

'I hardly think that the grief of bereavement ranks in the same league as walking out on your wife.'

He snorted. 'You're prejudging me, Lizzi. My wife

walked out on me, and took my two sons, aged six and four. I grieved, all right. I'll grant you it's not the same, but it's pretty damn traumatic, nevertheless.'

But Lizzi was cornered, and she wasn't in the mood to be conciliatory. 'At least you know she's still alive, walking around in the world. If you loved her, that would be enough—anyway, there's no smoke,' she muttered, and Ross sighed and ran his hands through his hair.

'Oh, yes, I know she's alive—alive and well and in another man's bed. That takes some getting used to, Lizzi. I dare say I was at fault too, but no more than any other junior hospital doctor struggling to establish a career. At least your husband left you reluctantly, without destroying your belief in yourself as a lovable human being! Hell, I'm too tired for this. We'll argue about it another time. Thank you for the coffee.'

With that he was gone, and she let herself back inside. Her legs were trembling slightly, and she felt shaken and upset.

It wasn't improved by finding her mother waiting for her in the kitchen.

Lizzi sighed. Here we go, she thought. She wasn't wrong.

'What a charming man, Lizzi. He doesn't seem the least bit cross with you.'

She snorted. 'He is now.'

'Oh, Lizzi, how have you upset him?'

'He was prying about David. It serves him right.'

Her mother sighed. 'I don't know how you expect to find another man if you——'

'I don't want another man! I'm quite happy the way

I am! Nobody suggests you should rush out and find yourself another husband, so why should I?'

'Because, my dear, you're twenty-nine years old and I am fifty-four. I've had my family, I'm confined to a wheelchair and I have very little to offer. You, on the other hand, are young, beautiful, and you have your whole life ahead of you. You need a partner, Lizzi. You aren't whole any more. You need the love of a good man to make you complete.'

Her heart gave a sudden thump. 'You have an overactive imagination, Mum,' Lizzi said, and changed the subject firmly. 'What was it Jean told you to think about?'

'Oh, nothing much,' her mother replied airily, waving her slender hand. 'Just a little trip we thought we might take—and don't change the subject. We were talking abut Ross.'

'No, we weren't! You were trying to marry me off!'

'Quite! Now, about Ross——'

'No, Mother!' Lizzi said firmly, and changed the subject again.

However, later that night, lying restlessly in bed, she raised her fingers to her lips and touched them lightly. How odd, she thought, that they should still tingle. An image of Ross sprang to mind, and a wave of heat washed over her body. Was her mother right? Did she need a man's love? Then the heat drained away, insignificant in the aching emptiness. She'd had that love once, and lost it. Did she dare try again?

She thought again of Ross's words. Did he really think he was unlovable? That was crazy. He was warm, generous, funny, professionally extremely competent and thorough, quick to anger but even quicker to forgive, as she had found out. All that, coupled with his striking good looks and lazy sensuality—no woman in her right mind could fail to love him, Lizzi thought, and then the heat washed over her again, leaving her trembling with fear and anticipation—and surprise.

Surely not? No! She couldn't fall for him—she wouldn't allow it! To expose herself to that terrible agony of loss all over again—no, it was out of the question. Anyway, it was probably just hormones. She would ignore him, she decided, and he would give up.

But what if he didn't? What if he persisted in unravelling her, as he had put it? What would she do then? What she had done in the past—freeze him out. They gave up quickly, usually. Men hated rejection; it was bad for the ego. She didn't want to hurt Ross, and for that reason it would be best to act immediately, before he felt he had a hope. Her mind made up, she turned over, punched the pillow into shape and fell instantly asleep.

It was another busy morning. Jennifer Adams had had a restless night and was in pain, and Oliver came up to see her and adjust her drugs.

'Ross was in a towering paddy last night, by the way,' he commented. 'Seems someone wrapped his new car in the car park yesterday.'

Lizzi blushed, and he eyed her speculatively. 'Was it you?' She nodded, and he cleared his throat. She thought it sounded suspiciously like a muffled laugh. 'Have you seen him yet?'

'As a matter of fact, I have, we sorted it out last night, but I'd be grateful if you didn't spread it around.'

'Trust me,' he said with a wicked twinkle, and left the ward for Outpatients. As she turned round, Lizzi almost fell over Dan Haig, the houseman. He was smirking.

'Haven't you got anything to do?' she snapped, and marched into her office.

Ross was thankfully absent, as it was his list that morning, and he was tucked away in Theatre, leaving her in peace.

At twelve Lucy Hallett came into the office and told her that Jennifer Adams wanted to talk to her. She made her way to the little side-ward, and perched on the edge of the chair beside the bed.

Jennifer was young, only twenty-three, and understandably frightened and unhappy. Her soft brown eyes were puzzled, and she was pale. She gripped Lizzi's hand.

'How's Peter?' she asked. 'Nobody seems to know how he's getting on. Someone told me he might be moved to Addenbrookes, but not why, and now I can't seem to get any further information out of anyone. I have to know how he is!'

'I'm afraid I don't know,' Lizzi answered honestly. 'I'll do my best to find out.'

'Why would they take him to Addenbrookes? That's where they take the head injuries, isn't it?'

Lizzi remembered that Jennifer's husband had been the one in ITU the previous morning, who was to have been moved as soon as he was stabilised enough. 'That's right. I understand he did have head injuries, which is why they were moving him, but I have no idea of the extent of the injuries, or even if he's been transferred yet. I'll find out for you. And don't worry, you'll soon be feeling better and then you'll be able to see him.'

She left the room and went back to her office, troubled. Why hadn't the consultants told Mrs Adams about her husband's condition? She flicked through the Kardex, but there was no relevent note on it. She phoned ITU, and the sister there told her that Mr Adams hadn't been transferred.

'Oh, good. He must be less severe than at first thought, then?' Lizzi speculated.

'Unfortunately not. He's too fragile to move. He had a massive depressed fracture and they did a craniotomy, but his intra-cranial pressure's risen and he's leaking CSF from his nose. We're ice-packing him now to induce hypothermia—that might reduce it, but he's been on the life-support since they admitted him. They're about to repeat the brain-stem test, but I think it's just a formality. He's got no reflexes and his pupils are fixed. I'll keep you posted.'

Lizzi thanked her and hung up. It was worse, far worse than she had anticipated. She went back to Jennifer, put on a bright face and smiled.

'He's still here, and they're running some more tests. I'll let you know the results as soon as we have them.'

She went up to lunch, and poked a salad around her plate for ten minutes before giving up and taking her coffee into the lounge. Ross was there, slouched in a chair with his feet on a table, laughing with Oliver and his wife Bron. They looked up and waved her over to them. There was a cluster of people around the bulletin board, and as she walked across the room she noticed nudging and giggling aimed in her direction.

Her brow twitched into a puzzled frown. 'What's that all about?' she asked.

'I take it you haven't seen it yet, then?' Bron said, trying to hide her smile.

'Seen what?'

Ross hauled himself up the chair and grinned. 'The cartoon. Some wise guy's decided to lampoon us.'

'Us?' she squeaked. 'What us?'

'You and me.'

'I didn't know we were an us!'

His mouth quirked. 'Give me time,' he murmured, so quietly that only she heard. She blushed instantly, and he smiled knowingly.

'So,' she repeated, 'what us?'

'Go and look,' Oliver suggested, grinning.

Just then there was a shout of laughter from the vicinity of the board, and a tall black man wove his way between the tables and dropped into a chair beside Lizzi.

'Hello, Dr Marumba. Seen something funny?'

'Oh, Lizzi, it's a classic! I love it! The Ice Maiden and the Abominable Snowman!' He slapped his leg and rocked with laughter.

She glanced up at the board again. The crowd around it had faded away, and she just had to know—excusing herself, she stood up and crossed the room quickly.

There, in the middle of all the notices about job vacancies, training courses and voluntary aid programmes, was a cartoon showing her little car squaring

up to Ross's Daimler. Both cars were growling and
pawing the ground, and Lizzi and Ross were standing
on the top of the cars like charioteers, she looking
aloof and victorious, he unmistakable with his shock of
white hair, standing with his feet apart, brandishing a
huge sword, challenging her.

The caption read,

Ice Maiden Targets The Abominable Snowman—
does this herald a new ice-age? As the Yeti brings
Arctic conditions with him, so Bizzi Lizzi tackles the
invader. Has Sister Killjoy met her match, or is she
in her element? Watch this space for further devel-
opments in the Cold War!

'Good, isn't it?'
Lizzi jumped, and turned to glare at him. 'Good?
Ross, are you out of your mind?'
'Not at all. You have to learn to take a joke. I like
the symbolism!'
'Symbolism?'
'Of the sword. Impressive, isn't it?'
She blushed furiously as his meaning sank in. 'Don't
be absurd!'
He grinned that infuriating lop-sided grin. 'I'm rather
flattered, actually.'
She ignored him and, snatching the cartoon down
from the board, she walked away, her cheeks still
touched with fire. Abandoning the remains of her
coffee, she stalked back to the ward, incensed with
rage, and marched into her office.
Lucy Hallett was just jotting down a note. 'Oh,
Sister, I'm glad you're back. ITU just rang. They got

the results of the brain-stem test on Mr Adams, and he's been certified brain dead. He had a massive intracerebral haemorrhage, apparently, as well as the fractures. They've turned off the machine. The neurologist's just coming up to tell his wife.'

Her anger drained away, leaving a huge void in its place. She stared sightlessly out of the window, remembering another time, another place, another young woman whose life had been shattered. . .

'Sister? Are you all right?'

She turned back to Lucy, her eyes wide, and pulled herself together visibly. 'Thank you, Staff. I'll deal with it. Perhaps you and Staff Nurse Tucker could do the drugs?'

Lucy nodded and left, and Lizzi sank down at the desk. Oh, God. Poor Jennifer. Most people would be able to distance themselves from the tragedy, and most of the time Lizzi could, but this case—these *people*, she corrected herself, were just too close to home. She felt cold, so cold, as if icy fingers were clutching at her heart.

When the neurologist tapped on her door and came in, he found her busy working at her desk, her face outwardly calm—at least, Lizzi hoped she looked calm. Inside she was a seething mass of dread, but she was used to putting on a front, and today was no different from many others.

She got up and went with him, and watched his gentle but systematic destruction of the young woman's life with as much distance as she could manage.

When Jennifer started to cry, he stood by helplessly waiting for Lizzi to comfort her, and eventually she did, moving mechanically to cradle the young woman against her taut chest while she thought vainly of sea breezes and long walks in the country, how she would reconcile the following week's duty rota with everyone wanting Easter off, and whether she needed to go to the supermarket on her way home. There was also the nagging question of her car. It would need to go into the garage at some point for inspection by the insurance company's assessor, prior to being repaired—good, her tears were subsiding. Lizzi eased away from her, smoothed her hair back from her face and smiled.

'I'll get you a cup of tea, and I'll find a nurse to come and sit with you.'

She stood up, led the neurologist out of the room and went back to her office.

'Does she really need a cup of tea?' the neurologist asked with a quirk to his eyebrows.

She shrugged. 'Universal panacea. They don't often want it, but drinking it gives them something to do. Did you want something?'

He shook his head, raised one eyebrow at her rather curt dismissal and left.

She wanted to scream, to sob and rage and throw herself down and weep for hours, but it was impossible. After she had detailed a nurse to take Mrs Adams a cup of tea and sit with her, she did the next best thing and took some junior nurses round the ward for a teaching session. She was unreasonably hard on them, and several times they exchanged glances of commiseration with each other, but they all stuck it out and came away wiser.

Lizzi went into her office and closed the door,

ignoring their comments behind her back. They all knew she was in a grotty mood, but of course they thought it was because of the cartoon. It would never occur to them that the cool, detached Sister Killjoy could possibly feel any emotion because someone had done something as everyday as *die*!

She heard her door open and shut, but she didn't lift her head.

'Hiding?'

The voice was soft, Scots and full of teasing good humour. She put down her pen with a sigh.

'No, Mr Hamilton, I'm not *hiding*. I'm *working*, unlike some people. If you want to kill time, perhaps you'd find somewhere else to do it!'

Her glare wiped the grin off his face, and he dropped into the chair opposite and steepled his fingers, then lifting his head he gave her a level look.

'I have very good reasons for being here, *Sister* Lovejoy,' he said, with just the barest of emphasis. 'It may have slipped your attention that you have six patients on your ward who were on my list this morning, and who are now in your care, but it hasn't slipped mine. I've come to see how they are, and I wondered if you would care to come round with me. That is,' he said with a heavy layer of sarcasm, 'if it isn't too inconvenient!'

Lizzi blushed under the implied rebuke. 'It is never inconvenient. You're welcome to come and see your patients at any hour of the day or night. I've finished what I was doing, anyway.' Ages ago, she thought, but pushed back her chair and stood up and joined him at the door.

As they went round she watched him, conferring with the nurses specialing the post-op patients and examining the patients themselves, asking how they were feeling and giving them details of the operations and how they went; Lizzi thought again what a good doctor he was. He had that easy blend of charm and sincerity that put people immediately at ease, and he was never patronising.

So many doctors fell into the trap of treating their patients like idiots—his predecessor, for example—but her patients were very lucky in their two consultants, she admitted.

The round finished, they were passing the door of Jennifer Adam's room when they heard anguished sobbing, and the voice of a nurse trying to calm her.

Ross glanced at Lizzi enquiringly.

'Her husband died of head injuries. We told her just after lunch.'

He frowned. 'She's very distressed—has anyone written her up for a sedative?'

'No. Oliver's in Theatre, and his registrar hasn't turned up yet. I sent for him half an hour ago, but he was busy in a clinic. Goodness knows where the houseman is.'

'Young Haig? He's down in A and E. Want me to do it?'

She nodded. 'Would you? She could certainly do with it.'

'Of course.' They went back to the drugs trolley and he drew up five mg of diazepam. 'That should help her get through,' he said after giving the distressed woman the injection.

Lizzi said nothing. It would take more than one shot of diazepam, she thought grimly. The woman's distraught face swam into her mind, and she deliberately dismissed it.

'Any chance of a cup of tea?' Ross asked as they went back into her office.

'Sorry, I'm off duty now.' She smiled brightly at him, her control thin. If she didn't get rid of him and go home, she was going to fall apart very publicly.

'The PM report came through on Michael Holden, by the way,' he told her. 'I was right. Ruptured traumatic aneurysm of the aortic arch. He also had a skull fracture.'

'Congratulations,' she said shortly.

He caught her arm as she walked past him, and pulled her up against him.

'What's the matter? I thought you wanted him to die?'

'Don't be ridiculous. Let me go, please.'

'No.' His voice was firm but persistent. 'Tell me, Lizzi, what did your husband die of?'

'I can't see the——'

He trapped her chin with his fingers and tipped her head up so that she was forced to meet his eyes. The understanding and sympathy were nearly her undoing.

'Tell me,' he commanded softly.

'Head injuries,' she whispered, then, pulling her arm free, she grabbed her bag and fled.

CHAPTER THREE

'I'LL get it,' her mother called, and Lizzi turned off the shower, wrapped her hair in a towel and rubbed herself quickly dry. Who on earth was calling on them at this time of night?

'It's for you, darling, your nice Dr Hamilton,' her mother told her through the door. 'I'll take him in the sitting-room.'

'He's not my nice Dr Hamilton!' Lizzi muttered fiercely. She sagged against the wall and listened to the rhythmic squeak of her mother's wheelchair and Ross's firm, steady tread. What on earth was he doing here? It suddenly occurred to her that her policy of keeping him at a distance wasn't working very well, and that getting him to come to the house the previous evening was quite possibly one of the silliest things she had done in a long while.

She dragged on her robe, gave her hair a last rub and dashed for her bedroom, dressing hastily in jeans and sweatshirt and dragging a comb through her hair. She hovered at the dressing-table, eyeing her freshly scrubbed look and debating make-up, but then she caught sight of David's photo.

Was she mad? She was supposed to be discouraging Ross! Shutting the drawer with unnecessary vigour, she pushed her feet into her slippers and went into the sitting-room.

'Hello, Ross. What a surprise!' she said coolly.

He grinned and rose to his feet, undeterred by the chilling welcome. 'Last night you suggested we had another cup of coffee.'

'You declined,' she reminded him.

'No,' he returned, 'I took a rain check. I've come to collect, but with a difference.'

'A difference?'

He smiled slowly. 'I'm taking you to my house.'

'Oh, no!'

'Oh, yes. I have your mother's permission, and you've already washed your hair so you can't use that as an excuse——'

'But it's still wet——'

'So go and dry it. You've got three minutes.'

'It will take much longer——'

'Ten, then. I'll talk to your charming mother.'

Lizzi swivelled her eyes round to her mother. 'Tell him I don't do this sort of thing!' she pleaded.

'Oh, I did,' Mary Reed said with a smile, 'and we both agreed it was a dreadful shame. Now come on, Lizzi, be a little welcoming! The poor man doesn't know a soul, and he's lonely.'

'Yes, I am, and I think it's jolly unfair of you to be so mean!'

She glowered at him. His easy imitation of her mother was so gentle that she hadn't noticed, but Lizzi had.

'Pretty please?' he added, managing to look at once both wounded and devastatingly sexy.

She laughed despite herself. 'You win—this time! Give me five minutes.'

In fact it was nearer ten, because she changed her mind and applied a quick touch of make-up—just for her self-respect, of course!—and changed into a dress, and then back out again into her sweatshirt and jeans, jazzing it up with a colourful scarf. Not even her self-respect could call for a dress just to go and have coffee in his house!

He rose to his feet as she went back into the sitting room, swept her with a look of wholly masculine appreciation, and turned to her mother.

'I'll have her back safely by ten, Mary.' He winked, kissed her hand and escorted Lizzi out of the door with a hand on the small of her back. It felt—well, it felt—good grief! Warm, firm, intimate, and very, very good. She moved away and pulled on her coat.

'I'm ready when you are,' she said, and cursed her voice for its breathless note.

He raised an eyebrow and his lips twitched, and he muttered something under his breath which could have been 'I should be so lucky', but she wasn't sure and didn't dare ask!

He ushered her into the car, and as she settled into the soft cream leather he climbed in beside her, turned the ignition key and pulled silently away. Soft classical music flooded the car and made conversation unnecessary, for which she was profoundly grateful. Something was happening between them, and she felt powerless to stop it.

As they went through the outskirts of the town, she watched the sure, confident movements of his hands on the wheel—nothing hurried, nothing hasty or ill-judged. She would like to watch him operate, she thought.

As the car headed almost silently out into the country and the velvety blackness of the night closed in around them, she got the strangest feeling that they were the only two people in the world. There was something terribly intimate about the confines of the car; she could smell the faint scent of leather, and a lemony tang that drifted across from him, released by the warmth of his body. She had to hold herself rigid to overcome the urge to lean closer.

By the time they turned into his drive, her senses were thoroughly tantalised. The subtle smell of his cologne, the strong, capable hands with their light scatter of dark hair, the slight shift of his thighs—raw, animal magnetism drew her to him, and she felt utterly helpless. Like a fly caught in a spider's web, she could only wait and see.

He slid out from behind the wheel and came round to open the door for her, tutting at her because she had got there first.

'You have to allow me to be chivalrous,' he chided gently, his voice brimming with laughter. Taking her elbow, he helped her out and then she was standing, looking at the most extraordinary house she had ever seen. There were very few windows facing them, and she thought at first it must be rather dark inside, but then he explained.

'The other side is nearly all glass, overlooking the valley. You can't see it now, of course, but there's the most spectacular view from most of the rooms. It's rather weird, but it provides what I need, and I like it,' he said, perhaps a little defensively.

'It sounds. . .interesting,' Lizzi said slowly, a smile spreading over her face. 'It's very unusual, isn't it?'

He grinned. 'It gets better, I promise.'

She looked around. The sprawling cream-painted building seemed to be single storey, and yet it wasn't. She was in the inside of an L, with one wing slightly raised above the level of the main span, rising to her left. They went towards the front door in the angle of the L, and entered the hall, which ran from side to side. Immediately on her left were some steps leading up, she supposed, to bedrooms, and on the right were several doors through an archway—the living-rooms, probably.

The most startling feature was ahead of her, lit by a floodlight which shone down a huge flight of paved steps before falling on still, blue——

'Is that a pool?' she asked, incredulously.

'Yes. That's one of the reasons I bought the house. The boys love swimming, and I spend so much time in Theatre that I need regular and acceptable exercise to keep me fit. Otherwise I'd get varicose veins and a dowager's hump!'

'What a gruesome thought!' she laughed. 'Is it heated?'

'Good God, yes! I wouldn't go in it if it wasn't. Do you want a swim?'

'What, now?'

He nodded, but she declined, tempting though it was. She didn't want him getting the wrong idea, and

somehow at night, with the velvet darkness all
around. . .

He led her under the arch and through some double
doors to the living area, which was on two levels. The
pine-panelled ceiling sloped down towards the far side,
where it met a vast wall of glass.

'Ross, it's spectacular!' she breathed.

He smiled self-consciously. 'Thank you. I fell in love
with it on sight. It's not much at the moment, but I
have ideas!' He laughed, and waved his hand. 'This bit
will be the dining-room when the furniture comes, and
the sitting-room's down here.' He led her down a few
steps at one side and into the lower room. There was a
cream leather rocker-recliner at one end, near a small
television, but otherwise the room was virtually bare
except for dozens of boxes stacked up all around and a
soft white rug by the fireplace.

'Books,' he said, waving expansively. 'Take a chair,
or should I say *the* chair? I'll light the fire and put the
coffee on.'

She slipped off her shoes, tucked her feet under her
bottom and sank back into the chair with a sigh.
'You're into cream leather, aren't you?'

He laughed. 'I've ordered a suite. It should be here
soon—it's dark green, like the car.'

She flinched, and he chuckled. 'I forgive you, Lizzi,
love.'

The fire caught, and he went out to the kitchen. She
could hear him making spluttering noises, and went to
investigate.

'I haven't unpacked the coffee machine yet,' he said
ruefully. 'I thought if I made the noises——'

She giggled, and the sound was so unexpected that she stopped, startled.

'Lizzi? What's wrong?'

'I haven't laughed like that—not since—oh, Ross——'

He opened his arms, and she fell into them with a tiny sob. He felt so strong, so *safe*! His arms were firm but gentle, keeping out the demons—it was so long since any man had held her and comforted her, and it felt so good.

She didn't realise she was crying until he lifted her face and wiped away the tears.

'Want to talk about it?' he said gently.

She shook her head. 'It was just seeing Jennifer Adams today—it was all a bit too close to home.'

'I know. That's why I came over. I thought it might help you to talk about it, but out of the hospital. I would imagine your staff all think you're as hard as nails and don't give a damn about Mrs Adams—am I right?'

She sniffed and nodded. 'I expect so. It's the impression I try to give—not that I don't care, but that I remain detached. Most of the time I get away with it, but when I have to deal with relatives—I suppose it's so much harder because I know just exactly what it is I'm doing to them.'

He hugged her, then let her go. The sense of loss was shocking. 'Coffee,' he said, and turned back to the kettle, making silly coffee-machine noises again to cheer her up.

They took the tray through to the sparsely furnished

sitting-room, and then he insisted she take the chair again while he sat on the floor by the fire.

'So,' she said, sipping her coffee, 'tell me your plans for the room.'

'Soft terracotta on the walls, warm cream carpet, and a wild jungle-print abstract at the windows. Lots of big pictures which will look good, I hope. They looked all wrong in my last house, but I love them, so they'll go up again even if they look hopeless!'

'No interior designer?'

He shook his head emphatically. 'It's my home, and I don't want any cold-blooded streamlined career-woman telling me what I like!'

Lizzi chuckled. 'They aren't all like that, you know.'

'Who? Interior designers, or career women?'

'Either, but I meant interior designers. David's sister is an interior designer, and she's really quite a decent human being.'

'The exception to prove the rule,' he said lazily, and stretched out in front of the fire.

For a while they sat in silence, watching the flames dance above the logs, and then Lizzi's mind returned to the humiliating episode of the cartoon in the coffee-lounge.

'What are we going to do about the phantom cartoonist?' she asked.

His brow twitched in a frown. 'Do? What can we do? I imagine it's one of the registrars having a joke—it's quite harmless, and I really don't think we can do anything unless he goes too far. That might be the end of it, anyway.'

She snorted. 'Not likely! It's happened before, two

years ago, and nobody found out who it was, although lots of people had their suspicions.'

'Did it get out of hand then?'

She chuckled. 'It depends whose side you're on! Not really, but I wouldn't like to be the target of such accurate barbs! It all blew over, and I suppose it was just a bit of harmless fun, but—I don't know, it's the second time in two days I've been called the Ice Maiden in my hearing, and. . .'

'Yes?' he prompted gently.

'It hurts,' she whispered.

He got up and came over to her, scooping her up from the chair and sitting in it with her sprawled across his chest.

'Why does it hurt?' he asked softly. 'It isn't true——'

'But they think it——'

'So show them they're wrong. Unbend a little—heavens, go mad and laugh from time to time!'

She giggled again, and his deep chuckle joined in. 'You see,' he murmured against her ear, 'it isn't so difficult.'

She lifted her head and his mouth came down and found hers unerringly. His lips were warm and firm and mobile, gently persuasive, and with a tiny ragged sigh she relaxed against him and allowed him to deepen the kiss.

When he lifted his head, his eyes were dark with passion and his breathing was rapid.

'They don't know how wrong they are, do they?' he whispered, and pulled her head down on to his chest so that she could hear the thudding of his heart under her ear. It matched the speed of her own, and she laid her hand flat against his breastbone so that she could feel it. The soft hair on his chest felt springy against her palm, and she eased her fingers absently between the buttons and threaded them through the curls.

He groaned gently. 'Lizzi, far be it from me to stop you, but do you have any idea what you're doing to me?'

She straightened instantly, as if a puppet-master had jerked her strings, and the flush of passion escalated into a full-scale blush.

He chuckled. 'Don't run away, love, you're quite safe. I'm not an adolescent seething with hormones.'

Speak for yourself, she thought, her emotions in shreds. Her hormones were raging out of control, and she was shocked to the core by the fact!

Easing away from him, she slid to the floor and knelt in front of the fire. She didn't need the heat, goodness knew, but somehow the hissing of the resin in the logs and the deep glow of the flames put everything back into perspective. It was just a simple little kiss, after all. Two adults together in an intimate setting—quite natural, expected, even.

Was that what he'd expected when he brought her here? Was he about to suggest——?

'I'd better get you home if I'm to keep your mother on my side,' he said with a trace of laughter in his voice, and she gave him a level look.

'You winkled your way into her good books remarkably quickly, Ross. My friends don't usually call her Mary.'

He raised an eyebrow. 'She told me to—and I

imagine your friends aren't encouraged to spend much
time with her—she reveals rather a lot, doesn't she?'

Lizzi's heart hiccuped. 'Such as?' She pretended
fascination with the flames.

'Such as the fact that your father was also killed in
the accident, and she lost the use of her legs. I gather
you felt guilty because you'd been ill and so weren't
with them, and had a difficult time coming to terms
with the fact that you were the only one to emerge
unscathed—except you aren't, are you? Not by a long
way.'

She was aware of him behind her, kneeling on the
rug with his thighs cradling her hips, his chest hard
against her spine. He wrapped his arms around her and
held her gently but firmly—safely.

'She talks too much,' Lizzi muttered defensively.

'Hush. Don't get prickly. Why don't you talk to me?
Tell me how you feel.'

She sighed and relaxed against him, giving in to the
temptation of his solid comfort.

'I'm much better than I was. At first. . .' She shivered at the memory, and his grip tightened reassuringly. 'I hated myself for a long while, but I had a
friend who put me in touch with a bereavement counsellor, and she was wonderful.' She shifted round in his
arms, so that she could see his face. 'How about you?
Are you better now?' She lifted a hand and touched his
face gently. 'I said some unforgivable things to you last
night. I suppose I hadn't really given the stress of
divorce a great deal of thought, but something you
said—do you really feel unlovable?'

He sighed. 'No, not really, not any more. I did—for

ages I couldn't understand why anyone would want to speak to me, much less love me.' He turned his face into her hand, and pressed his lips to her palm. He smiled sadly.

'I couldn't believe it when the boys told me that they loved me. It used to make me cry, and then I thought, "But they're only children, they don't count"—but they do, of course, and bit by bit I got my confidence back. I suppose I'm OK now, more or less. I'm content—I couldn't say I'm happy, but I'm content, and I know now that I'm not an evil person and I haven't failed Ann or the children.'

'But she left *you*! Of course you didn't fail her!'

He laughed, a short, self-deriding snort. 'You said yourself, there's no smoke without fire. I was so busy there were weeks when we barely exchanged civilities, never mind spent any meaningful time together. I suppose I could claim the pressure of work, but really our marriage was dying and I hadn't noticed. We were very young when we married, and we changed, as people do. She needed more from the relationship, not only more but *different* things. She was right to do what she did, and now I can see how happy she is with Andrew, but at the time I was stunned. I hadn't even noticed that things had got so bad. In fact, when she left me things were better than they had been, but the damage was done.'

He gave her a quick squeeze, then stood up, pulling her to her feet and thus ending the painfully intimate conversation before it went any further.

'Home,' he said softly, and she was glad to go.

Glad, because his frankness and honesty were

revealing more about him than she wanted to know—
and not enough. And soon it would be her turn. It was
time to call a halt.

Mr Widlake was returned to them from ITU the
following morning, and was looking much better. His
wife, sporting a colourful bruise on the side of her face,
sat with him most of the time. They asked about
Michael Holden, and Lizzi gathered that it was their
car that had hit him after he was thrown clear. They
were very distressed to hear that he had died, and she
was amazed at how concerned they were that they
might have caused his death.

Ross came down to discuss Mr Widlake's care and
treatment, and Lizzi mentioned it to him.

'How can they be so compassionate when he nearly
killed them both?' she pondered aloud.

'Some people are just not naturally vindictive,' he
said, and she pounced on it.

'Meaning that I am?'

He sighed. 'Of course not. But you are bitter, and
it's destroying you. You ought to let it go while there's
still time.'

'Time for what?' she asked, and even she could hear
the bitterness in her voice.

He eyed her speculatively. 'Time for you—time for
love—time for us?'

Her head flew up, and her eyes tangled with his.
'Ross, I——'

'Not now. I've got to get on. I'll take you out
tonight.'

'I'm on a split—I won't finish until nine.'

'That's fine. Let's go and see Widlake.'

She followed him out of her office, and tried not to think about the warmth of his arms or the feel of his lips. She didn't hear much of what he had to say, either, but fortunately he was called away before he could notice her distraction. Was he right? Was she really so bitter? And was her mother right to say that she needed a man—or just Ross? She cleared her mind of his distracting presence, chatted to the Widlakes for a minute and then gave the junior nurses a teaching session on monitoring and maintaining fluid balance.

Fortunately the day continued uneventfully until lunchtime, when Lizzi handed over to her staff nurses and left for the afternoon. She took the opportunity to go to the garage and get her car assessed for repair. After that she went to the supermarket and shopped, and took the food home in time for a quick cup of tea with her mother before returning to work.

'How's Ross?' her mother asked with studied casualness.

'Fine,' Lizzi replied, refusing to be drawn. If her mother wanted a blow by blow account of last night, she could sing! She blushed at the thought, and then caught her mother's eye.

'He's very taken with you,' her mother told her candidly.

Lizzi grimaced. 'And not just me. He thinks you're wonderful, too. You are a gossip, Mother!'

She smiled benignly. 'Just helping the course of true love, darling.'

She snorted. 'What true love? Really, you talk tripe

sometimes, Mum! Must fly. I'll see you after nine. Oh, no, I'll be late. Will you be able to get yourself to bed?'

'Of course, darling. Going anywhere nice?'

'I don't know,' she replied.

'Anyone I know?'

'Ross,' she muttered briefly, and avoided her mother's all-too-seeing eyes. 'I'll see you later.'

She dropped a kiss on her mother's smooth, unlined cheek and left for the hospital.

She knew something was wrong the moment she walked into the ward. There were raised voices from her office, and as she drew nearer she could distinguish Ross's angry tones and the more subdued tones of one of her junior nurses. She opened the door, slipped in and closed it behind her.

'Problems?'

'I'll say! This bloody stupid young fool has practically killed a patient with her ignorant interference, and now she tells me she didn't *think*! Would you *believe* it?'

She turned to the nurse. 'Nurse Winship, go and put the kettle on, please.'

'I haven't finished with her!' Ross growled.

Lizzi gave him a level look. 'Yes, you have. Off you go, Amy. I'll deal with this.'

She waited until the girl was out of her office, and then turned on Ross with barely concealed fury.

'How *dare* you discipline a member of my staff? If there is a problem on the ward concerning the conduct or reliability of one of the nurses, you take it up with me, please, not the nurse concerned! I will not have you ranting and raving and terrorising my girls, is that understood?'

'You have no idea of the seriousness of this situation, have you? You just——'

'Why don't you tell me?' she put in quietly, and sat at her desk, struggling to bring sanity to the situation.

Ross stalked over to the window, hands jammed in his pockets, and glowered at the glass. Finally he spoke.

'Mrs Avery—the woman who had the cholecystectomy on Friday—it seems her drain fell out during Sunday evening, and in all the chaos after the snow everyone was so busy that your young Amy Winship couldn't find out what to do, so she wiped it on a tissue and pushed it back in! I took it out on Monday, but she developed a slight temperature this morning, and by lunchtime she was raging. They called me down, and before I arrived she had a crashing drop in blood-pressure and started vomiting.'

'Good lord!'

'I'll say. She's got septic shock, Lizzi, and she could quite possibly *die*. Now tell me I overreacted!'

'Ross, I'm sorry——'

'Sorry? There'll have to be an inquiry—I would think we'll be lucky if they don't sue us.'

Lizzi frowned. 'Who did the op? And why did the drain fall out?'

Ross's face drew into a forbidding scowl. 'I intend to find out all I can, and you deal with Amy Winship, then we'll submit a report and it can go from there. Meanwhile Mrs Avery is on blockbuster penicillin and I've set up an IV line. We're running saline in fast to boost her fluids, and she seems to have stopped vomiting. Hopefully we caught it in time, but she's not feeling too grand.'

He shook his head in disgust.

'Ross, I'm sorry.'

He looked up at her, surprised. 'You? Why?'

'My nursing staff, my responsibility.'

'Nonsense. You weren't even on duty!'

'Even so, I should have foreseen the possibility and pre-empted it with tuition. I didn't, and I apologise.'

He studied her for a few seconds, and then his face softened slightly. 'Don't worry. Keep an eye on Mrs Avery, and I'll see you at nine if not before.'

'Ross, in view of this, perhaps it would be better if we didn't go out——'

'Why? I want to see you.'

'I don't think that's a good idea——'

'Why not?'

'I've just said——'

'Feeble excuses. I'll see you at nine in the main entrance.'

He tugged her close, grinned his lop-sided grin and lowered his lips to hers just as the door opened.

She jumped like a scalded cat and wrenched herself out of his arms, just in time to see the door closing softly. She looked up at him, and could have smacked the grin off his face.

'Did you see who it was?'

He chuckled. 'No, but I guess your reputation's shot.'

'Damn!' She sank to the chair, pressing her hands to her flaming face. 'How can you laugh?'

He sobered, and dropped to his haunches in front of her. 'Relax. I was kissing you, Lizzi. Anyone would think we were dancing stark naked in a fountain the way you're going on.'

She met his eyes, and the hunger in them reflected her own.

'See you at nine,' he whispered, and dropping a light kiss on her forehead, he left.

A few seconds later there was a knock on the door, and Amy Winship came in, looking chastened and upset. She had obviously been crying, and no doubt Ross had shown her the error of her ways in words of one syllable. With a sigh, Lizzi waved to the chair opposite.

'Amy, sit down and tell me all about it,' she said gently.

Ross was waiting when she arrived in the main entrance hall just after nine. She had quickly changed into a soft wool jersey dress she had taken back with her that afternoon, but her hair was still up and she was only wearing a touch of make-up. She hoped they weren't going anywhere too formal.

He smiled, and escorted her to her car without touching her, for which she was at once profoundly grateful and perversely disappointed.

'I'll follow you home and we'll go in my car—save you having to drive tonight,' he said as she slid behind the wheel. They made the changeover at the bungalow, and, after seating her in his car, he drove to a country pub with an informal but excellent restaurant. Instead of getting out, after he had parked the car he pulled a slip of paper out of his pocket, unfolded it and passed it to her, turning on the interior light so that she could see.

It was another cartoon, showing them tangled in a passionate embrace. The caption read,

> Cold War Hots Up. Abominable Snowman captures the Ice Maiden. Is this the effect of global warming, or just a temporary heat-wave? Watch this space for Yeti 'nother instalment!

Lizzi groaned. 'It was nothing like that!'

'You're right,' Ross commented, flicking off the interior light, 'I had my hands here——' he slipped them round her '—not here.' His right hand slid back and down her hip, cupping her bottom and pulling her towards him, while his left hand deftly removed the pins from her hair and threaded warm fingers through the tumbling curls. His mouth brushed hers lightly once, twice, before settling firmly against her lips with a soft sigh.

After a moment he shifted in his seat and groaned quietly. 'This wretched console—things were easier in my student days. I had an old Austin Cambridge with a bench seat!'

Lizzi giggled. 'That's the price you pay for success!' she teased. 'Anyway, aren't we a little old to be necking in cars?'

'Probably,' he agreed. 'Shall we go back to my place?'

She eased away from him, unsure how serious he was. 'I don't think so,' she replied carefully.

He gave a deep, rich chuckle. 'I was joking—just about! Come on, let's go and eat first.'

'First?' she said primly.

He opened his door, and in the soft light she could see the laughter dancing in his eyes. 'First—I can wait for dessert!'

'You're very confident!' She tried not to sound too repressive, but he was cornering her, and she felt threatened.

The laughter died in his eyes, and he reached out a hand.

'Not confident, just hopeful. I like you, Lizzi Lovejoy—I like you a lot. In time—who knows? Don't put the brakes on us now. Give us a chance to find out—please?'

Her heart in her mouth, she reached out and took his hand.

'I'll try—I can't promise, but I'll try.'

His fingers tightened on hers, and he pulled her gently towards him. 'That's all I can ask,' he murmured, and then his lips touched hers.

'We're necking again,' she whispered, moments later.

He laughed. 'So we are. Some people never grow up. Come on, lady, I'm starving. Let's go and eat.'

He leapt out of the car, ran round to her side and opened the door, pulling her out into his waiting arms. With a quick hug, he locked the car, grabbed her hand and ran with her through the light rain to the restaurant.

'Last one in's a chicken!' he yelled, and as they ran

laughing to the door, they almost cannoned into a young man and woman who were coming out.

'Evening, sir, Sister Lovejoy,' said an amused, gravelly voice.

Ross straightened and pulled himself together, but held on to her hand. 'Evening, James.'

Lizzi blushed and fumbled for something sensible to say, but by the time she had found it the couple were on the other side of the car park.

'What a time to bump into your registrar!' she said with a groan.

Ross chuckled. 'That's OK. It'll help to launch your campaign.'

'My campaign?'

'To show them you're human!'

Lizzi sighed. They might have found a more subtle method!

CHAPTER FOUR

THE restaurant was busy but not crowded, and they found a table tucked around the corner out of the way where they had an element of privacy.

Ross leant back in his chair, folded his arms across his broad chest and studied Lizzi across the table. 'Got your temper back?' he asked with a grin.

'Beast! What a time to be seen!'

Ross quirked an eyebrow at her. 'Are you ashamed to be seen with me?'

'No, of course not,' she denied quickly. 'It's just— well, I felt awkward—I mean, running like idiots, yelling "last one in's a chicken"—it's not very dignified—stop laughing at me!'

He tried—he did try, but somehow it didn't seem worth the effort, and then they were both giggling like teenagers. The waitress came, stood for a second and then said she'd come back later, which just set them off again.

'Ross, behave, they'll throw us out in a minute and I'm starving!' she protested, wiping her eyes and struggling with the laughter that rose like bubbles in her throat.

'We'll go and get fish and chips from somewhere and eat them in the car, then. I don't care. It's worth it just to see you laugh. I get the feeling you don't do it nearly often enough. Am I right?'

She felt the laughter drain away under his compassionate gaze, and she dropped her eyes. 'Since David died—I haven't been out much. If you go out with a man, all he wants to do is—well, they just have one-track minds, and if you go out with girls all they want to do is attract the men! And that's the last thing I want——'

'Is it?'

'Yes!' Her head flew up. 'Yes, it is, Ross. I couldn't—I don't want to get involved again, it hurts too much. Don't you feel the same?'

He shook his head slowly. 'Not any more. There was a time, just after Ann left me, when I went a bit mad. I had a string of brief and meaningless affairs just to prove that someone—anyone!—still wanted me, but,' he waved a hand expressively, 'they left me feeling even more alone, and, believe me, that hurts more than involvement. After a few months I gave up and threw myself into my work. I haven't ever really stopped since then, but now. . . Since meeting you, I think maybe there is more to life than saving other people's. Perhaps I'm ready to try again. God knows I don't want to be hurt, but nothing ventured and all that, and I'm sick of being on my own.'

The waitress came and took their order, and then he leant over and took her hand where it lay on the table-top.

'That's why it was so nice last night when you took an interest in my house. I bought it really with the boys in mind, and I moved down here deliberately to be near them at their school, but they don't give a damn what colour I paint the walls or which fabric I hang at the windows, so long as there's food in the fridge and water in the pool. It was really encouraging to get some positive feedback on the house. I was beginning to wonder what on earth I was doing there, rattling around that vast space all on my own. Having no furniture doesn't help either. Just me and the walls. . .'

He sounded so totally isolated that Lizzi's heart ached for him. At least she had her mother, and they took an interest in each other's lives. She felt intuitively that there was no one who really cared one way or the other about Ross, and that was desperately sad.

Turning her hand, she gripped his fingers and lifted them to her lips.

'I'm sorry you're so alone,' she said quietly.

He cupped her cheek, and she turned her face and pressed her lips to his palm.

When she looked up, his eyes were suspiciously bright and very intense, and she felt as if she was drowning in emotion. Then he checked it, reining it in visibly, and she dropped his hand and turned away as the waitress arrived with their order.

After that, they kept the conversation deliberately light, avoiding personal topics and sticking to hospital gossip and medical anecdotes as if by arrangement.

They avoided the subject of Mrs Avery and her drainage tube, neither of them wishing to spoil the evening with a reminder of such a contentious issue, and then all too soon it was closing time and he was dropping her off at home.

'Coffee?' she asked quietly, but he shook his head.

'I'll just see you safely in.'

Taking the key from her, he slipped it into the lock, stepped inside the door and took her in his arms.

'Thank you for this evening, Ross,' she whispered.

His head came down and his lips grazed hers. 'You're welcome,' he murmured, and then he kissed her, at first tenderly, then with a ragged groan he pulled her hard against his body and his mouth fastened on hers with a desperate hunger.

By the time he lifted his head, her legs were like jelly and her heart was thrashing like a wild thing.

'Goodnight, sweetheart,' he whispered shakily, and let himself out. She laid her fingers on her lips where his had been and closed her eyes, listening to the gentle burble of his car as he drove away.

Slowly her heart settled down and she locked the door and made her way to bed.

As she sat at her dressing-table removing her make-up, the picture of David caught her eye and she paused, her hand suspended half way to her face. Had she felt the same when he kissed her? Maybe—and maybe not. It was so long ago she could hardly remember.

With a troubled sigh, she reached out and touched his face, but all she felt was cold glass, and if she closed her eyes all she could see was Ross laughing, his eyes sparkling with humour, his mouth lifted in that lop-sided grin that was so particularly him—no, she couldn't remember any longer how she had felt in David's arms, and it saddened her to think that their love had been so transient.

She almost put the picture away, but it was all she had left of him now the memories were gone, and it seemed so cruel. A slow tear slid down her cheek, and then another, but she let them fall. All that was left of her raging grief was a gentle sorrow, and she owed him that.

Turning away at last, she climbed into bed and lay for ages staring at the ceiling, trying to banish the image of Ross that formed on her eyelids every time they closed, but he wouldn't be banished, and in the end she let him stay, allowing her eyes to drift shut and her body to remember the feel of his as he held her close. Cradled in the memory of his arms, she sank gently into a tranquil sleep.

In the morning Mrs Avery was much better, her fever abated and her fluid balance restored. Ross was operating, and Lizzi hardly saw him in the morning except for a brief visit for a coffee halfway through his list. In the afternoon he popped into the ward to check on his patients, and spared Lizzi a few moments in her office over a cup of tea. However they were seldom without interruptions, and there was no opportunity to talk except in the most general vein.

One thing she did find out was that the operation on Mrs Avery had been performed by Ross's junior registrar Mitch Baker, supposedly under the eye of the previous consultant. However, he had been detained over lunch on the day of the operation, as it was his last day, and had been conspicuous by his absence. Mitch had done the list alone and unaided, and as he was apparently qualified to do so no one had turned a hair.

'Thank God he did it as well as he did,' Ross said

with a sigh, and Lizzi agreed fervently. Lack of supervision from more senior staff was a constant problem in hospital life with the consultants spread so relatively thinly on the ground, but it was a problem they tried hard to combat at the Audley.

'What about Amy Winship?' Ross asked, but Lizzi couldn't shed any more light on the incident.

'She told me what she'd told you—she said she realised afterwards that it was a stupid thing to do, but she hoped nothing would happen. It's only her first ward—she's just barely out of PTS, Ross, and if it hadn't been for the snow she would have asked someone, I'm sure. It's such a shame. Perhaps she'll get away with a ticking off from the CNO as Mrs Avery's making progress now.'

Ross nodded. 'I hope so. She seemed genuinely devastated by what she'd done. I'm sorry I laid into her, but it's the sort of mistake we just can't afford.'

'It won't happen again, I can assure you,' Lizzi said with a slight smile. 'The poor child is terrified to do the TPRs at the moment!'

Just then Ross's bleep sounded and he picked up her phone and checked in with the switchboard.

Lizzi busied herself at her desk, but something in his tone caught her attention, and she found herself listening despite her better intentions.

'Easter Monday? No, I can't really see a problem, but I'll be working—no, I don't suppose it matters. Not the damn dog—stick it in kennels. Why not? It wrecked all the carpets in my last house, that's why not, and I'm just not having it—fine. Thank you. OK, Ann, I'll expect you on Monday week. Bye.'

He returned the phone with a sigh, and leant back in his chair with his eyes shut.

'Your wife?'

He opened one eye. 'My ex-wife. They're going on holiday for a week and want me to have the boys.'

'And the dog?' she added.

He grinned mischievously. 'I declined.'

'I noticed!'

'Eavesdropper!'

'It's difficult not to be.'

He levered himself out of his chair. 'I'm going to find your Mitch Baker and teach him a thing or two about inserting drains in abdominal incisions. What are you doing later?'

'The washing.'

'Really?' His face brightened. 'Want to do mine?'

'No, thank you.'

He grinned. 'Pity. I'm moving into the residence tonight, because the painters start tomorrow on my house, and I can't stand the smell of new paint. I wondered if you'd like to give me a hand to bring my things over.'

'What, your toothbrush and a change of underwear? Can't you manage it all by yourself?' she teased.

He leant across the desk and grinned wolfishly into her face. 'Of course I can manage my underwear, but I thought you might like to come and help me!' he said suggestively.

She put her hand in the middle of his chest and pushed him away.

'Sorry, Casanova, you'll have to cope on your own! I'll be up to my elbows in suds.'

'My heart bleeds,' he said with a chuckle. 'It's room thirteen, in case you change your mind.'

'Yes, well, it'll be unlucky for you tonight,' she replied blithely, standing up and moving symbols on her wallchart.

'Only tonight?' His voice was very close behind her, and as she turned she found herself trapped in his arms.

His mouth was laughing, but his eyes held a serious light that made her heart trip and catch.

'Don't push, Ross,' she said breathlessly, and his arms dropped immediately.

'Sorry. I didn't mean to crowd you. I'll see you tomorrow.'

He left, and she felt suddenly churlish—and abandoned. How ridiculous! She didn't want him to push her, after all—did she?

She made herself do the washing, almost as a punishment, when she knew she could be spending the evening with Ross and having fun—because it would have been. Every time she saw him he drew her out further, made her laugh more and longer.

And it was addictive. Perhaps she ought to stop seeing so much of him, she thought as she shoved wet clothes from the washing-machine into the tumble-drier. Yes, that was it. Stop seeing him. That way. . .

That way, she wouldn't be laughing at silly jokes, and running through the rain, and kissing him goodnight—oh, lord. That goodnight kiss——!

She slammed the door on the tumble-drier and

twisted the knob viciously. She wouldn't think about it, she wouldn't!

She made a coffee and sat down with her mother in front of the television.

'Not seeing Ross tonight?' she enquired casually.

Casually, my eye, Lizzi thought. 'No. Not tonight. I was just helping him pass the time while he found his feet. . .' Liar, she chided herself.

She looked up and found herself skewered by her mother's gimlet eye. Funny how everybody thought Mary Reed was such a gentle, absent-minded little soul. Lizzi supposed being in the wheelchair was largely to blame, but although she was aware of her mother's physical limitations Lizzi had never doubted her mental acuity.

'Actually he's moving into the hospital for a few days while the decorators go through his house.'

'What's it like?' her mother asked, and then watched with a satisfied expression while Lizzi went into passionate and intricate detail in her description.

'Sounds impressive,' her mother said.

'I suppose so.'

'It certainly seems to have impressed you, darling,' Mary added.

Lizzi shrugged, trying for neutrality. 'It's OK in its way, I suppose,' she said dismissively.

Her mother raised an eyebrow and turned back to the television. Lizzi glanced at her watch. Nine-fifteen. Perhaps Ross would be at the hospital by now. Maybe she'd ring him.

She went into the hall, conscious of her mother's eyes tracking her every move, and shut the door firmly behind her. She dialled quickly before she could change her mind, and was put through immediately.

'Hamilton,' a gruff voice announced, and she swallowed. 'Hello?'

'Hi. It's Lizzi. You're there, then?' she said inanely, and could have kicked herself.

'Uh-huh. I'm here, I think. Or I might be in Edinburgh again. I don't know, the lumps on this mattress seem awfully familiar!'

Lizzi smiled. 'What are you doing?' she asked, her voice softening automatically with affectionate amusement.

'Oh, just lying on the bed reading a book. I could have done with some company, but you know how it is—everyone seems to be doing their washing tonight!'

'Everyone?' She tried to sound outraged, and failed dismally.

He chuckled. 'Everyone except a certain scrub nurse who was standing so close to me in Theatre this evening I thought she was trying to get inside my clothes!'

Lizzi giggled. 'She probably was.'

'Hmm. Well, she failed. However I can't guarantee I'd be so unfriendly if the circumstances were different.'

Lizzi froze, shocked by the sudden rush of jealousy. 'How different?'

'Well,' he said slowly, and she could hear the bed shift as he moved, 'if it was you, for instance.'

She relaxed, and he must have heard her sigh, because she heard his soft laughter. 'Oh, Lizzi, you're so easy to tease! Trust me, sweetheart,' he said in a voice like warm syrup.

'I'm not sure that's wise,' she muttered.

'Maybe not, but it could be a lot of fun,' he countered.

'Ross, I've told you——'

'I know. I'm leading you astray again, aren't I? Or trying. Don't take me so seriously.'

'Are you telling me you're trifling with my affections?'

'Lord, no! I loathe trifle. All that cold custard— yuck!'

She giggled, then fell silent.

'I wish you were here,' he said softly.

'I wish I was, too,' she murmured, so quietly she didn't think he would have heard, but he had, as his next words showed only too clearly.

'Come over. I'll sneak you in.'

'Ross! Don't be ridiculous!'

She could see his frustrated, lop-sided smile. 'Just a thought. You're probably right. Well, if you won't join me, we'd better get off the phone before my circuits overheat. Goodnight, Lizzi, love. Sleep tight, and thanks for ringing.'

'You're welcome. Goodnight, Ross.'

There was a loud, smacking noise in her ear. 'What was that?' she laughed.

'A goodnight kiss. See you, princess.'

The phone went dead, and Lizzi stared at the receiver for a second or two before returning it to the rest. He was so silly, so deliciously light-hearted—but was that all? Was he really just a shallow playboy? She didn't want to think so, and every now and again he gave her a glimpse of emotional depths that startled her with their intensity.

Take last night, for instance, when she had said she was sorry he was so alone. Those weren't the eyes of a man who chose emotional independence.

So that left her the other choice. He was serious about her, and growing more so.

She was hard put to work out which terrified her more.

CHAPTER FIVE

FRIDAY morning was bedlam. Oliver was doing his list, and Ross was on take for emergencies. He had operated on a man with a strangulated hernia during the night, and was in Theatre again with an acute appendix. There was a suspected perforated duodenal ulcer next in the queue, and goodness knew what the morning would bring.

By coffee-time Lizzi was run ragged. Two of her junior staff were off, which just spread the workload more heavily across the remaining nurses—herself included. And she still hadn't conquered the rota for the Easter weekend!

She met Ross on his way into coffee, and as they walked in together a crowd standing by the bulletin board turned as one, looked at them and turned away with a knowing grin.

'Not again,' she muttered out of the corner of her mouth, and heard his deep chuckle in her ear.

'Looks like it. Let's go and find out.'

As they approached the board, the crowd parted like the Red Sea and melted away.

'Oh, aye. Here we go. "The Three Snowshoes". Funny, I could have sworn the pub was called The Three Horseshoes. "Stop Press. Definite signs of global warming in Suffolk as Ice Maiden turns to slush. Further abominable changes are on the menu, but is this Yeti 'nother false alarm? Watch this space!"' He chuckled, and traced the picture with his finger. 'I like the way you're melting all over me!'

Lizzi snorted. 'You should be so lucky! Take it down!'

'Spoilsport. He's only having fun.'

She started taking out the drawing-pins. 'At my expense. Well, at least we know who it is now.'

'My expense too, and I don't think it is James. I watched him doodling over someone's notes yesterday, and, frankly, he can't draw for nuts. So we still don't know.'

They joined the others, the cartoon safely in Lizzi's possession.

'Again?'

Reluctantly, Lizzi yielded up the cartoon. The others passed it round, chuckling and grinning.

'What were you doing?' Jesus Marumba asked.

'Running through the rain.'

'Mucking about like kids,' Ross corrected. 'Shrieking and giggling and holding hands and generally having fun.'

All eyes turned to Lizzi, and she felt the blush rising up her chest, then her neck, and flooding her face with colour.

'He's an idiot,' she said lamely. 'He leads me astray.'

'Huh!' Oliver commented. 'It's damn well about time *someone* led you astray. God knows enough people have tried and failed!'

She ignored that. 'It's just so *public*! I hate it. We can't do anything without being watched. If we only knew who it *was*!'

'It's going to get worse, too, now I'm living in,' Ross said as they walked back to the ward together. 'You'd better not come up to my room, even in broad daylight with the door open! God only knows what the guy would make of it!'

'Perhaps we ought to see less of each other,' Lizzi said quietly. She had been thinking that ever since the previous evening's phone call, and the cartoon had just strengthened her feelings.

'Blow that,' Ross replied firmly, 'and I'm not sneaking around meeting you in secret, either! We can't stop whoever it is having their fun, but we can make sure we don't do anything too outrageous.'

'I have no intention of doing anything even slightly outrageous!' Lizzi said indignantly.

Ross smiled slightly. 'Pity. I was looking forward to restraining you! Are you free tonight?'

She shot him a startled look. 'What for?' she asked suspiciously.

His mouth twitched in a grin. 'I have a slight transport problem, owing to circumstances beyond my control. My car's in the bodyshop now, as I don't need it, but I'd like to have a look at the house and see how they've got on. How do you feel about picking up a Chinese take-away and running out there this evening?'

'All right, but I don't think——'

They turned into the ward just as she was about to decline the food, and Mitch Baker appeared beside them.

'Sir, I wonder if you could have a look at Mr Widlake?' he asked, and they went off together.

A few minutes later Ross popped his head round the

treatment room door where she was checking CSSD stocks. 'No panic. One of his stitches is a bit inflamed, so I've told Lucy Hallett to remove it. Could you keep an eye on it? Oh, and,' he grinned mischievously, 'pick me up at seven from the residence. Make sure nobody sees you coming in!'

He closed the door before she could retort, and left her feeling more confused than ever. He just wouldn't take no for an answer, but perhaps it was because her 'no's were a bit half-hearted. She felt she was being swept along on a tidal wave, out of control, with a fifty-fifty chance of being deposited gently on a warm sunny beach or flung headlong into the sea defences.

Knowing her luck, it would be the sea defences! She sighed and started counting packs again.

As the seven o'clock news started on the radio, Lizzi pulled up outside the doctors' residence and glanced around her. Suppressing a giggle, she turned up her collar, put her sunglasses on and pulled her hair round her face. Then, with another quick glance around, she let herself out of the car and ran for the door.

Ross's room was down the hall on the left, and she tiptoed down the hall and tapped on the door.

'Come out with your hands up!' she hissed, and he flung the door open and dragged her through it.

'Get in here, you lunatic! I've been watching you through the window. Why are you doing Bonnie and Clyde impressions?'

She laughed. 'It's so ridiculous! All this sneaking around.' She took off the sunglasses, unbuttoned her coat and bounced on the bed. 'Oh, good grief! Lumps? It's dreadful!'

He chuckled. 'Tell me about it—I had to sleep on the thing! Come on, let's go before someone catches you looking like the Mafia!'

He opened the door and hustled her out into the corridor just as a crowd of young doctors turned the corner.

Several eyebrows twitched, and Mitch Baker smiled knowingly at them.

'Have a nice meal,' he said, so innocuously that Lizzi almost didn't believe the flash of mischief she saw briefly in his eyes.

Ross's arm tightened warningly about her shoulders.

'Thank you, Mitch. I'm sure we will. You're on call, aren't you?'

He nodded.

'I've got my bleep with me—don't hesitate to contact me if you get anything complicated like an appendix!'

With a wicked grin, Ross wheeled Lizzi out into the car park and managed to squeeze his considerable length into the passenger-seat before the laughter bubbled over.

'Ross, you are naughty. Poor lad——'

'Poor lad damn well ought to know better. He was just winding us up—I wonder if he can draw?'

Lizzi paused in the act of turning the key. 'Do you think it's him?'

'Don't know and I don't care. Let's get that take-away, I'm starving.'

In the end they went to look at the house first, and

then took the meal back to the residence because the house smelt so awful.

'Are you sure this is a good idea?' Lizzi asked dubiously as they let themselves back into his little room.

He gave a dismissive shrug. 'Let him do his worst. I really don't care what he says about us. I would have thought propriety will keep him more or less in line. What did you think of the house?'

'Coming on well. They've certainly made a good start,' Lizzi commented as she opened the foil containers.

He put two plates beside her on the chest of drawers. 'You dish up; I'm going to see if I can find Mitch and check everything's all right.'

He left her, and once everything was on the plates she stuck her head out of the door and called, 'Right, come and get it!'

A group of doctors stopped in their tracks, turned and grinned. 'Really?'

She fought the blush. 'Not you, idiots!'

Ross stuck his head out of a doorway further down the corridor. 'Did you want me?'

Lizzi nearly choked. 'Your supper's ready,' she said tightly, and almost shut herself in the door in her haste to get away from the amused eyes of the housemen.

Ross came in chuckling, and she shot him a fulminating glare over her shoulder. 'Did you have to phrase it quite like that?'

In answer he wrapped his arms around her and rested his chin on her shoulder. 'You never did reply.'

Her insides quivered at the touch of his warm, hard

hands against her hips, tugging her back against his solid bulk. She pushed him away. 'It's getting cold.'

'Speak for yourself,' he said, and his voice was rich with laughter. 'This mine?' he asked, reaching over her shoulder and picking up a hugely heaped plate.

'Take your pick,' she said, offering him the much more scantily clad one.

He snorted, picked up a fork and climbed on to the bed, sitting cross-legged at the head. 'Come on, then,' he mumbled through a mouthful of food, 'or it'll be cold, and I understand even ice maidens like the occasional hot meal.'

She threw a prawn cracker at him, which he caught and ate.

'Hey, you were supposed to throw that back!' she cried.

He grinned wickedly. 'You didn't tell me the rules.'

She sniffed. 'Knowing you, you would have moved the goal-posts anyway.'

It was difficult to smirk and eat at the same time, but he managed it. Lizzi couldn't stay cross with him, and found herself laughing before long.

When they had finished eating, he cleared away the plates and took them out to the kitchen, returning a moment later with some coffee.

It was too hot to drink and somehow without knowing quite how it happened Lizzi found herself lying full length beside him on the bed, her head cradled in that perfect hollow just below his shoulder, one leg hitched up and rested across his thighs.

'Mmm,' she sighed.

'Mmm indeed.' He shifted against her so that they

were lying face to face, and his hand rested against her hip. With the gentlest pressure he closed the gap, easing her against him.

Her breath caught in her throat. 'Ross, I don't think——'

'Don't think. Just feel.' His lips came down on hers and teased them gently, and she sighed and relaxed against him for a delicious moment before finding the presence of mind to move away.

'Ross, no! I can't——'

'Hush.' He pulled her close again, but this time held her gently in a passionless embrace, stroking her hair with one large hand while the other rested quietly against her back.

Gradually her heart slowed, and she stopped fighting the warmth and allowed herself to enjoy the simple human contact. God, it had been so *long*! She had almost forgotten how good it was to hold someone and be held. She wriggled closer.

'Steady, love. I'm only human,' he murmured against her hair.

'I know,' she replied softly, 'that's what's so good about it. I'd forgotten.'

He pressed his lips to her brow. 'Tell me something?'

'What?'

'Has there been anyone since David?'

She shook her head slightly. 'No. I never thought there would be, either, but. . .'

He seemed to tense, and then relaxed deliberately. 'But?'

'I'd forgotten,' she repeated. 'Warmth, human contact—not the lovemaking, that's nothing really, but the holding, the safe feeling about being held—the caring, really, I suppose—I'd forgotten how good it was. It's the price you have to pay for it, though—I don't know, maybe it's just too high.'

He was silent, his breath teasing her hair, his chest rising and falling beneath her hands.

'Ross?'

He paused so long she thought he must have gone to sleep, but then he sighed.

'If it's right, you don't count the cost. You can't. Somehow, whatever the price, you have to pay it.'

'No!' she breathed, her heart racing.

'Are you telling me that David wasn't worth the pain?'

'Oh, God, Ross, that's unfair!'

'Is it?' He rolled away. 'If you'd known in advance what was going to happen, would you have married him?'

She bit her lip. How could he ask that? And how could she answer? A tiny sob broke from her throat and he rolled back and wrapped her hard against his chest.

'Hush, love, I'm sorry. It's none of my damn business. Don't cry. . .'

He rocked her gently, holding her close and shielding her from the pain; quite when the comfort turned to passion she didn't know, or care, but it did. His lips found hers and they parted for him, softening with desire as he threaded his fingers through her hair and groaned against her yielding mouth.

The phone was shocking in the semi-darkness, the sound a harsh intrusion in their passionate cocoon.

Ross lay stunned for a second before disentangling himself from her and rolling over.

'Hamilton,' he muttered, his voice gruff and ragged. 'OK, I'm on my way. Thank you.'

He cradled the receiver and swore softly.

'Emergency?'

'Uh-huh. Mitch Baker wants a hand.'

She wriggled up to the top of the bed and picked up her cold coffee.

'Here, drink this.' She passed him his cup. Seconds later there was a knock at the door and Ross opened it, just far enough.

'Sorry to disturb you, sir, but there's an appendix I'm not happy about. She's being prepped now, but I'd appreciate some assistance.'

His brows drew together in a scowl. 'Mitch, this had better not be a hoax,' he said warningly.

In the mirror over the basin opposite, Lizzi saw Mitch's impassive face. As she watched, his eyes met hers and held, and again she saw a flicker of mischief before he controlled it.

'No hoax, sir.'

'OK, I'll see you up there.' He shut the door firmly, and Lizzi slumped against the pillows with a sigh.

'That's blown it.'

Ross frowned at her. 'Blown what?'

'He saw me—in the mirror. It'll be all over the hospital by the morning. I'm going home.'

She swung her legs off the bed and reached for her coat at the same time as Ross. Their hands met and he pulled her into his arms.

'I'm sorry, Lizzi,' he groaned. 'I'll shut him up.'

She laughed weakly. 'Don't bother—it'll probably do my campaign a power of good.'

He chuckled against her hair. 'That all depends on how far you want to change your image!'

'Yes, well, I'd better get out of here now if I want to keep any vestige of decency!'

With a quick kiss on his cheek, she let herself out and ran lightly down the steps to the car park.

Damn Mitch Baker, she thought, but Ross's gentle warmth stayed with her longer than her irritation at the registrar, and lulled her into a deep and restful sleep.

She was on a late the following day, and by the time she arrived at the hospital Ross had been round the ward and left. Oliver handed her a note, and she quickly slit the envelope and scanned it, smiling to herself.

He raised an enquiring eyebrow.

'Ross,' she said unnecessarily. 'The appendix last night turned out to be ruptured, and peritonitis had set in. We wondered if it might be a hoax.'

She explained about his parting shot to Mitch, and Oliver laughed. 'Teach him to patronise his registrar!' he said.

'We did wonder—do you suppose he could be the cartoonist?'

Oliver shrugged. 'Maybe. Did you by any chance have a take-away last night?'

She gave him a quizzical look. 'Yes—a Chinese. Why?'

'Did Mitch know about it?'

She nodded slowly. 'Yes, he heard Ross ask me, and he told us to enjoy it. Yes, he knew. Why?'

'It might explain the cartoon,' Oliver said enigmatically, and left her puzzled.

What cartoon? She yanked the door open. 'What cartoon?' she asked.

Several people turned round and stared, some with laughter in their eyes, others frankly puzzled.

'On the board,' Oliver replied. 'You'll see it later.'

She couldn't get away until three-fifteen, by which time there was a good crowd round the bulletin board in the coffee-lounge. As she went in, Ross detached himself from the usual crowd and made his way over to her.

He looked wonderful in old, faded jeans and a sloppy sweater, his hair tousled and his skin touched with the outdoors.

'Been for a walk?' she asked.

'Uh-huh. Get my note?'

'Yes, thanks.' She smiled. 'Have you been waiting long?'

He grinned and picked up two cups of tea. 'Long enough. The cartoon's a lulu, by the way.'

Oh, lord! She had forgotten in the pleasure of seeing him again.

'Let's have a look,' she said with resignation.

They walked over, and once again the grinning crowd faded away as they approached.

Lizzi clapped her hand over her mouth and stifled a shriek. The cartoonist had done himself proud. There was a picture of the interior of a restaurant, showing Lizzi lashed to a huge dining table, and Ross standing over her sharpening a knife. The menu was propped up on her chest and read,

Tibetan Take-Away. Stir-fried Breast of Ice Maiden with Chilly sauce; Wanton Skin in Sweet and Sour; Battered Snow-Balls Tibetan-Style; Yeti Fritters in Syrup.

The restaurant had a sign over the door which read, 'No. 13 Yeti's Diner'. Ross's room-number.

'Get *rid* of it!' she whispered fiercely.

He chuckled. 'I like it. Some of the items sound very tempting!'

She blushed. 'Yes, especially the battered snow-balls!'

'Ouch!' He winced and laughed. 'What are you doing with all the drawings, by the way?'

She glared at him. 'Taking them home where they're safe. What do you expect me to do, save them all up and auction them at the League of Friends summer fête?'

'It's a thought.' His lips twitched. 'I'd just hate to see them destroyed. They make a rather lovely documentary record of our courtship!'

'Courtship?' Her voice rose an octave, and she tugged out the drawing-pins and folded the cartoon up and slipped it into her pocket. 'Is that what you call being caught necking by one of your team every other minute and being publicly humiliated by some lunatic with a vivid imagination?'

He put the tea down on the table and leant over her shoulder, grinning mischievously. 'Of course I'd be able to court you much better with a car at my disposal, but since someone wrapped it——'

Her elbow caught him under the ribs, and by the time he had got his breath back she was sitting down demurely drinking tea.

'That was unkind!' he groaned.

'You deserved it. I've apologised enough, I refuse to be made to eat crow for the rest of my life!'

He looked at her oddly. 'The rest of your life?'

She blushed and looked away. 'Just a figure of speech.'

You could have heard a pin drop. In the deafening silence, he caught her chin and turned her face back to him. 'I think I could get to like that figure of speech,' he said quietly.

Her breath caught in her throat. The other people round them started talking brightly, covering the lengthening silence that stretched out between them.

They were totally unaware. They could have been on Mars for all the notice they took of their surroundings.

He means it! Lizzi thought with panicky dread. He really is serious. Then he was talking again, and she dragged her mind back into gear.

'Tomorrow? No, I'm not on duty.'

'Come with me to the house. Bring swimming things, and we'll spend the day together. It'll be fun. Please?'

She chewed her lip. 'I ought to spend the day with my mother——'

'I'd be lying if I said she was welcome, but if that's the only way I'll get you, bring her.'

She chuckled. 'That'd keep you on your toes!'

He shot her an amused look. 'You reckon? I think if

I dragged you off to my lair I'd have your mother's whole-hearted approval!'

'You're probably right,' she sighed. 'All right, I'll come. I'll pick you up at ten.'

She spent the rest of the day wondering how she had let herself be talked into anything so foolish, and the whole of the night looking forward to it.

CHAPTER SIX

'Ross, it's gorgeous!'

Lizzi turned round and round in the middle of the sitting-room and spread her arms wide with delight. 'Oh, it's going to be wonderful! I can see it now!'

He chuckled. 'You must be clairvoyant! Once the carpet's down and the furniture's here towards the end of the week it should start to look like home. Then I can get the pictures up—I miss them!' He caught her hand as she turned and tugged her up the steps towards the bedrooms.

'Come and see the rest. Apparently they've nearly finished.'

The master bedroom was huge, with one wall almost totally glass and looking out across the pool to the valley. The walls had been painted a soft white, and Ross explained that he wanted a simple look, an uncomplicated room where he could relax. 'I'll do a lot of work here probably, and I wanted something undemanding.'

'What's your furniture like?' Lizzi asked, trying to picture the room.

'Big! Pine, mainly, but the bed's cherrywood and enormous—it's one of those French things with curly bits on the sides and posts at the corners.'

Her eyes widened. 'Is it antique?'

'Uh-huh. I picked it up in Provence, and had to

arrange shipping, which was horrendous! It's so big, but it's incredibly comfortable. After the last few nights, I'm really looking forward to getting it back!'

Lizzi stood at the window, basking in the warm sunshine that streamed through the glass. He sounded so full of boyish enthusiasm, and it made her heart ache for him that he had no one to share it with. How she wished it could be her, but it was out of the question. If only she dared, but if she allowed him to get close to her——

She felt him behind her, felt the warmth of his breath tease her cheek. 'Penny for them,' he murmured.

Wordlessly she turned into his arms and hugged him hard.

'Hey, what's that for?' he whispered against her hair. 'Lizzi?'

'I'm fine,' she mumbled through his shirt, then pushed him away. 'How about that swim?'

He gave her a searching look. 'OK. Your things are in the hall. Change in here; I'll use one of the other rooms.'

He brought her bag in to her and left her in peace with her tangled emotions. As she undressed and pulled on her swimsuit, she wondered what she had let herself in for. Talk about out of the frying-pan into the fire! Suddenly the legs of the suit seemed higher cut, the top lower, and the bits between altogether too revealing! Strangely, in the crowded atmosphere of the public baths or on a sun-drenched beach it seemed perfectly respectable. Now—now, good grief!

She caught her lip between her teeth as she saw him running lightly down the steps to the pool, his almost naked body sleek and tanned, smooth-muscled and graceful, like a cat's. He bent and rolled up the bubble-cover, and then turned and waved.

'Come on down,' he called, and, taking a deep, steadying breath, she walked out of the room, down the short flight of stairs to the hall and out into the sunshine.

He waited for her at the bottom of the steps, watching her descent with a warm smile in his eyes. Not by a flicker did he betray any interest in her figure, and she felt a curious mixture of pique and relief. She wished she were as unaware of his body!

A soft tangle of dark hair, in such contrast to the silver-grey mass on his head, curled in tempting profusion across his broad chest, narrowing down over the ripples of his abdomen to disappear beneath the narrow black trunks that were all he wore. Beneath them, his long, straight thighs were scattered with more of the same soft curls, and his bare, well-shaped feet were planted squarely on the paving. As she reached him, his eyes swept once over her body and returned to mesh with hers, their expression unreadable.

'Bit different from last Sunday,' he said casually, and held out his hand. She took it, unsuspecting, and with one smooth movement he picked her up and threw her into the water.

She spluttered to the surface, but he had disappeared from the side and the first sign of him was the strong band of his fingers snaking round her ankle and tugging her under again. They came up laughing, splashing one another and playing like seals until their muscles ached and they turned on their backs and floated in the mild sunshine.

'You don't play fair,' she said idly, drifting quietly beside him.

'All's fair in love and war,' he returned, a smug smile on his face.

'Is that so?' She reached out a hand, placed it in the middle of his taut abdomen and pushed hard.

He jack-knifed and found his feet in the shallow water, standing over her with his hands on his hips, water streaming off his shoulders and running in rivulets through the tangle of dark curls that clustered on his chest.

'Cheeky,' he said mildly, and, hoisting her over his shoulder, he carried her up the steps and out on to the patio area. There he lowered her to her feet, sliding her slowly down his body so that the rough hair on his chest grazed against her thighs, imprinting them with an indelible memory. Her hands clutched his shoulders, the smooth, cool flesh like living marble beneath her fingertips.

Achingly slowly, he lowered her the last little bit so that her toes touched the ground and the water streaming off their legs mingled intimately at their feet.

Beneath the cool skin she could feel his warmth, feel the core of heat that burned within. Its flames flickered now in his eyes, trapping her, helpless, and a little moan rose in her throat, half fear, half anticipation.

Then, as quickly as they had come, the flames were gone, and his hands slid down her back and over her hips, easing away, leaving her.

'Temptress,' he said softly, and moved away, picking

up a towel and handing it to her before scrubbing himself vigorously with another.

She shivered in the slight April breeze, and he came over and wrapped her in the towel, rubbing her body firmly all over to blot the water off her skin while she stood numb, remembering the imprint of his body against her own.

'Come on,' he said at last, 'let's go in and get dressed, then we can go for a walk.'

She didn't think her legs would hold her, frankly, but just then didn't seem to be a good time to mention it. His face was impassive, but as she looked up she met his eyes, and the heat scorched her clean through to her bones.

For the rest of the day, they avoided physical contact and concentrated on keeping busy. They walked across the valley, coming back via the village and having lunch in the pub, then in the afternoon they unpacked some of the books in the sitting-room and arranged them on the shelves that covered one wall. As the sun sank in the sky they decided to call it a day and headed back towards the hospital.

As they approached, Ross touched her shoulder.

'Find somewhere to stop—somewhere where we can talk.' His fingers slid under her hair, teasing the strands apart, kneading her nape gently.

She shivered and he glanced keenly at her. 'Cold?'

She shook her head. 'No. No, not cold. I just— you. . .' She trailed off, unable to explain.

But he nodded anyway, as if he understood. 'We need to talk, Lizzi,' he said quietly.

She found a deserted car park and stopped the car in

the shelter of an old tree in the corner. Turning off the engine, she sat in silence staring straight ahead, her heart pounding. What did he want? He had been distant all day, ever since that moment by the pool— but then, to be fair, so had she. So what did he want? An end? Or a beginning?

'Look at me,' he murmured.

She drew in a deep breath and turned her head, and his hand came up and brushed the hair away from her cheek, tucking it behind her ear with a tender gesture.

'That's better, I can see you now.' He searched her face, his eyes serious, and then he dropped his hand and looked away. 'What do you think of me?' he asked, so quietly she wasn't sure she had heard right.

'What do I think of you?'

'Uh-huh. I mean, do you trust me——?'

'Of course I trust you! Why shouldn't I trust you?'

His eyes swivelled back to hers, and he gave an expressive shrug. 'Today, at the pool—you seemed afraid. I'd never do anything to hurt you, Lizzi.'

It was her turn to look away. 'I wasn't afraid, exactly. More. . .'

'Terrified?' he supplied, smiling tenderly.

She gave a breathless little laugh. 'I just—we were— oh, Ross, I was. . .'

His fingers traced the line of her cheek, the blunt tips warm against her skin, brushing her with fire. 'So was I. So I need to know what you feel for me.'

She swallowed. 'Feel?' she breathed. God, all she could feel was his fingers trailing a path to her heart.

'Feel. I know it's only been a week, but you know

enough about me now to know if you want to find out more.'

'I—yes, of course. I mean, I hardly know anything——'

'But you want to?'

'I—oh, yes. Yes, I do. I really like you, Ross. I'd like to get to know you well, to be your friend——'

His groan cut her off. 'Stop there, Lizzi, and let's get one thing perfectly clear. This relationship is going one of two ways, and friendship is only a small part of it. I know it's too soon to talk about love, but I have this almost biological urge to get to know you better. You're with me in my thoughts every waking moment, and I dream about you at night. I can't get you out of my head, and I'm damned if I want to! But when I saw the look on your face—Lizzi, I could have wept for you. Why are you so afraid? I thought you felt the same way, but I suddenly realised that you don't.'

His hand slipped under her hair and his fingers soothed her nape hypnotically. 'Talk to me, love. Tell me how you feel. I need to know.'

She sighed and dropped her head forwards, allowing him to lull her with his gentle hands, and then she straightened and looked at him. His eyes were unguarded, and he looked desperately vulnerable.

'Oh, Ross, I don't want to hurt you, but I can't cope! You're going too fast for me—I can't handle it. It's been so long, and so much has happened to change me—I'm just not used to showing my feelings. I'm not sure I can. I don't know if I can accept them myself, never mind share them with anybody else.'

He studied her, his face, usually laughing, so serious

now. 'Please try. Just think out loud. I'll never use what you tell me as a weapon.'

'OK.' Her voice was quiet, so quiet that he had to lean towards her to hear, but she made herself talk to him. 'I don't think you want to be alone any more, do you?'

He shook his head. 'I don't want to make another mistake, but I'm ready to share my life again.'

She nodded. 'I thought so. That's very difficult for me to deal with, because I know I never could. Apart from anything else, I have my mother to consider, and I could never her let her down, but I'm not sure I want to see you with anyone else either! I love being with you, and I feel I owe you so much—you've shown me how to laugh again, and all the bits of me that were frozen up inside have started to thaw. In a way it's wonderful, but in another way, it hurts. I've had to face a lot about myself, about the impression I give people that I'm uncaring—I'm not, I just care too much, and it rips me to bits, but I daren't show it. It makes me too vulnerable.'

He sighed. 'I'm vulnerable too, Lizzi. Things hurt me just as much. You just have to find a way to defuse the emotion. With me, I exercise—swimming, running, walking—but you, you bottle it all up inside and let it go on hurting you in private.'

'At least it doesn't affect anybody else.'

'But it does—it's affecting me now! If you didn't feel the way you did, do you know what we'd be doing now?'

Her eyes widened slightly. 'No. . .'

'Yes, Lizzi.'

'It's too quick——'

'Not for our bodies. They've been calling out to each other since the moment we met.'

She flushed and dropped her eyes. 'Ross, please——'

'It's true! Why can't you admit it?'

'Don't be angry!'

'I'm not angry.' He leant across and took her hand in his. 'I'm not angry, Lizzi, I'm frustrated. I want much more from you than you're giving me at the moment—possibly more than you'll ever be prepared to give me. If that's so, then you've got to tell me before I get in any deeper.'

'What *do* you want from me?' she whispered.

'Everything. Your mind, your heart, your body—all of them open to me, unguarded, honest.'

'Oh, God, no, Ross!' Her heart raced with nameless emotion, and she moaned softly and clutched his hand. 'Ross, I can't——'

'Try, Lizzi, for us? I want us to have a chance to find out if we can make it work, because I think we could, given time.'

'Can you do that? Give me time? Ross, I'm so scared——'

'Don't be scared. I'll be here.'

'Not if it goes wrong. Not if you die——'

She pressed her hand to her mouth, catching the sob and holding it in. Her heart was crashing against her ribs, and she could feel the panic rising, coming up to choke her. Then Ross's big hands were on her shoulders, pulling her into his arms, and he was soothing her, stroking her hair and murmuring reassuring nothings against her ear.

Then he eased her away, kissed her softly and smiled with such tenderness that she felt her eyes fill.

'Take all the time you need. I've got my answer now. You wouldn't get so upset if you didn't care what happened to me.'

You're wrong, she wanted to scream, it's me I'm worried about, not you, it's me, and how I'll cope when you're gone! But instead she found herself agreeing to take it slowly, to see less of each other outside the hospital.

'I'm having a party next week, on Saturday night. Will you help me organise it? I can't get any caterers in because it's Easter weekend and they're all busy with weddings, so I thought I'd fling a few things together and buy a couple of cases of wine and just let everyone get on with it, but I could use a hand if you aren't working.'

'No, I'm not working. Not on Saturday, anyway. I am on Good Friday and Easter Sunday, but nobody seemed to want Saturday off.'

'Great.' He grinned at her. 'You'd better take me back now. I've got a long list tomorrow and I want to look in on my patients tonight to reassure them. Are you on tomorrow?'

She shook her head. 'Lucy Hallett and Linda Tucker are on for the morning, and Sarah Godwin and Ruth Warnes are on in the afternoon. I'm not back until Tuesday lunchtime.'

He touched her cheek gently with a fingertip. 'I'll miss you. Will I see you tomorrow evening?'

'Ross, you said you'd give me time——'

'But I won't see you—oh, all right! But I'll be thinking about you.'

'I won't know about it, though.'

He grinned. 'But you will—I've told you!'

She smiled, despite her determination not to. 'Tease!' She started the car and drove back to the hospital, dropping him off outside the residence.

He opened the door, leant over and kissed her firmly on the lips before getting out. Then he leant back down, his large frame filling the doorway, and grinned. 'Have a nice weekend, Sister Lovejoy. I'll be thinking of you. I'll see you on Tuesday. Thanks for your company and the lift.'

Then he shut the door and sauntered off with a jaunty wave. As she started the engine and pulled away, she saw Mitch Baker and Lucy Hallett, arm in arm, threading their way through the car park. They raised their hands and waved, and she waved back, gritting her teeth. That was the trouble with hospital life, she thought, no privacy. Still, it would be better this week if they weren't going to see each other.

Her heart gave a funny little hiccup. How silly, she thought, you're pleased that he's giving you more room—aren't you? But suddenly she wasn't quite so sure.

During the week she hardly saw Ross, and never alone, and she was astonished at how much she missed his company. She could tell every time they met that he was biting his tongue, holding himself back, but she didn't know how to tell him that she didn't want that much room!

Anyway, by the time the cartoonist had had another go she thought perhaps they were doing the right thing. In the absence of any further material, he had resorted to a few illustrated Yeti jokes, and almost every day another one appeared.

They triggered a spate of other jokes aimed mainly at Ross, all of which he bore good-naturedly. On Wednesday they were sitting in the coffee-lounge when Jesus Marumba joined them, chuckling quietly to himself.

Ross raised an eyebrow, and Jesus grinned.

'How do you sterilise a yeti?' he asked.

'I give up,' Ross replied with a sigh. 'How do you sterilise a yeti?'

'Melt his snowballs,' Jesus laughed.

Ross groaned. 'You're worse than my kids!' he complained mildly.

Lizzi shut her eyes with a sigh.

'If I hear one more snowball joke I think I'm going to scream!'

'Did you hear the one about the yeti who——?'

Lizzi and Ross bombarded Jesus with paper napkins. He ducked and came up grinning. 'One more?'

'No!' they said in unison, and he sighed and picked a soggy ball of paper out of his coffee.

'I can't see why you're being so hyper about it.'

Ross laughed. 'That's because it's not you!'

'Oh, but it was! Two years ago our anonymous friend picked on Oliver and me, and did a series on the black and white minstrels. That was before Lucy and Bron captured us and stopped us racketing around together. It all died a death in the end, but it got pretty tedious.'

Ross frowned. 'Was Mitch Baker around at the time?'

Jesus drew his eyebrows together in thought, and then nodded. 'Yes, I think so. He would only have been a houseman, but yes, he was around. Why? Do you think it's him?'

Ross shrugged. 'Might be. He seems to crop up in all the most unlikely places. We thought James seemed a likely candidate at first——'

'James Hardy? Your senior reg?' Jesus shook his head. 'No. He wasn't here two years ago, and, believe me, I recognise this hand!'

'We'd dismissed him anyway—he can't draw to save his life, so he's a non-starter. No, I think I'll set Mitch up—get him out to the party on Saturday and see what happens. Are you and Lucy coming?'

'Try and keep us away! Lucy's itching to see the house—I have a sinking feeling that we might be about to move to the country!'

Lizzi left Ross giving Jesus directions, and went back to the ward. Mrs Turner, the woman who had had the ruptured appendix on Friday night, was vomiting again, and Lizzi was concerned about her. She had meant to mention it to Ross at coffee, but what with one thing and another—when he arrived on the ward the woman's condition was worsening, and she rang the switchboard and asked them to page Ross.

Mitch Baker appeared and she asked him to have a look at her as he was there.

'Vomiting?' he said, puzzled. 'I wonder why? I put

her back on a light diet yesterday because she seemed better.'

'Did you get bowel sounds?' Lizzi asked.

'Yes—I'm sure I did. What did she have to eat?'

Lizzi checked the notes. 'Thin soup and toast for lunch, and shepherd's pie for supper. Who gave her that?'

Mitch sighed. 'I'll go and have a look. If she's got a paralytic ileus the yeti'll kill me!'

He walked off, her notes in his hand, and Lizzi stared after him. The yeti? She shrugged. Everybody knew about the cartoons by now, so using Ross's nickname was no indication of guilt, but still, it did seem to come so naturally——

Her phone burbled, and she picked it up. 'Surgical; Sister Lovejoy speaking.'

'Hello, you gorgeous thing. You paged me.'

She smiled. 'Hello, Ross. Mrs Turner's vomiting— Mitch put her on a light diet yesterday and she doesn't seem to be tolerating it very well. He's gone off in a muck sweat to see if she's got a paralytic ileus——'

'I'll murder him!' he bellowed.

'Mind my ear,' she chided gently, 'and by the way, I think he's expecting it. He told me the yeti would kill him!'

'I'll fix the young rascal. Keep him there, I'm on my way up.'

Lizzi took one look at Mrs Turner and went out to the treatment room to prepare the trolleys for gastric aspiration and intravenous infusion. There was no doubt about it, she was showing all the signs of a paralytic ileus and Mitch had been too hasty putting her back on to solids. She wondered how Ross would react.

She didn't have to wait long. He tracked her down in the treatment-room and his scowl was a beauty.

'Poor Mitch!' she murmured sympathetically.

'Humph! What about Mrs Turner? The man's a menace—he should be struck off! Have you got all the stuff ready? We'll aspirate her first, and then when she's more comfortable we'll get some fluids into her.'

'All here,' she said with a wave at the trolleys.

'Right, let's get on with it, because every time she throws up she strains her stitches and the last thing we need is a burst abdomen!'

Lizzi suppressed a smile and followed him out with the aspiration trolley. On the way she collared Amy Winship.

'Bring the other trolley and come into Bay Two to Mrs Turner, please, Amy. You can assist.'

When she arrived at the unfortunate woman's bedside, Mitch was hovering uncomfortably and Ross was palpating the abdomen with gentle fingers.

'Right, there's a lot of fluid to come off, and we'll also have to leave a flatus tube in situ for a day or two until things get moving. Let's have her sitting up.'

Together they helped her into a sitting position and put gloves on, and Lizzi opened the Ryle's tube pack and held the tube up against Mrs Turner, marking the length to her stomach with a strip of tape. Then she lubricated the tube, and passed it to Ross.

'Just try to relax, Mrs Turner, and swallow a few times to help the tube down,' he said gently, and then,

using her own movements to assist, he quickly inserted
the tube through her nose and down into her stomach.

Lizzi attached the syringe to the end and drew up
the contents of her stomach, emptying the syringe into
a measuring jug and repeating the procedure over and
over again until the tube failed to yield up any further
fluids.

'Better?' she asked quietly, and Mrs Turner nodded.

'Oh, much. I still feel very blown up, but not nearly
so sick. Oh, I did feel bad!'

Ross squeezed her hand. 'Often happens, Mrs
Turner. It'll soon settle down again, but we'll have to
empty your stomach every fifteen minutes for the next
few hours and we'll also put up a drip again to get
some fluid into you the easy way!'

Mrs Turner smiled weakly at him. 'Thank you, Mr
Hamilton. I'm sure I'll be fine.'

'Oh, you will, I guarantee it. Now let's get this drip
set up.'

Within a very few minutes the drip was up and
running and the flatus tube had been inserted to relieve
the distension in her static bowel, and Amy Winship
was detailed to stay with Mrs Turner and monitor her
pulse and respiration, aspirate her stomach every fifteen minutes and record the volume, and generally
keep an eye on her.

On the way out of the cubicle Ross crooked his
finger and called her over.

'If anything falls out,' he said, wagging a finger at
her, and Amy blushed.

'I'll call you at once, sir.'

He grinned and winked. 'You do that, Amy.'

Lizzi bit her lip and went quickly back into her office, followed by Ross.

'You tease!' she murmured.

'Mmm.' He pulled her close and kissed her. 'I've missed you.'

'I've missed you, too. What are you going to do to Mitch?'

'Don't know. I'm more interested in what I'm doing to you.'

She pushed him away, just as Mitch Baker came in.

'Ah, *Dr* Baker,' Ross drawled softly. 'Just the man I wanted to see.'

Lizzi left them to it.

CHAPTER SEVEN

WHEN Lizzi arrived home that afternoon, she found her mother sifting through clothes in her bedroom.

'Hi,' she said brightly, dropping a kiss on her mother's cheek. 'What are you doing, sorting out jumble?'

Then she took a closer look at the garments, and her brow creased.

'Don't frown, dear, it's very ageing. Actually, I have something to tell you. I'm going away.'

Lizzi moved a jade-green silk blouse off the end of the bed and sat down—hard.

'Where——?' she croaked, and then cleared her throat and tried again. 'Where are you going? Who with? Why?'

'Yorkshire, with my painting group, because I want to,' her mother replied firmly. 'There's a watercolour weekend in a converted country house, and one of the group has had to drop out. If I don't go, they lose their group rate—either that or the person dropping out has to pay anyway, and the place would go begging, which does seem such a shame, don't you think, darling?'

'Me, think? *You* need to think—how will you manage the stairs? Who will dress and undress you? How on earth will you manage?' Lizzi's voice was rising, and she forced herself to calm down and try logic. 'Have you really considered all the ins and outs?'

Her mother smiled benignly. 'Of course, darling. I'm

not a complete imbecile, you know. I've only lost the use of my legs, not my mind!' Her rebuke was very gentle, but it stung nevertheless.

'I didn't think you had,' Lizzi replied, 'but how will you manage without me?'

'Jean will be there, and the place is fully equipped for the disabled—goodness, how I hate that word!' She threw a pile of underwear on the bed and wheeled over to her wardrobe. 'What do you suppose I'll need in the way of dresses? My legs look so thin now, I'd far rather wear trousers, but I suppose I ought to dress for dinner—what do you think?'

Lizzi, in truth, didn't know what to think. However, she might have guessed that Jean was in on it. She and Mary Reed had patently been hatching something when Jean had brought her back from the last class. She helped her mother select a couple of dresses that would answer for most occasions and travel well, and then laid them out on the bed.

'When are you going?'

'Tomorrow afternoon. Jean and I are going in Edward's car, with Molly.'

Lizzi's make-the-best-of-it smile slipped. 'Edward?'

It didn't seem possible, but Lizzi was sure her mother blushed. Certainly she made herself busy at the dressing-table collecting toiletries, and avoided answering for a moment or two.

'He's one of the group,' she replied eventually.

Lizzi eyed her mother keenly. 'Is he married?'

'Widowed, I believe. Darling, would you get me down the green suitcase from the top cupboard?'

Lizzi knew an avoidance mechanism when it hit her

on the nose—she should, she was an expert on them. But she got the suitcase down nevertheless, and packed it, all the time eyeing her mother surreptitiously.

'Would you stop looking at me as if you're counting my marbles?' her mother requested mildly, and Lizzi sighed.

'Sorry. It's just so unlike you to go off and——'

'Have fun?' her mother supplied. 'Elizabeth, I have sat here in this house for seven years and felt sorry for myself. Enough is enough. I am going to get on with the rest of my life. I'm sorry if you don't approve, but I'm afraid that's the way it's going to be.'

'Oh, Mum, it's not that I don't approve! I hope you have a lovely time. I was just worried that you would find it awfully difficult to cope.'

'So what? It won't kill me, will it? Lizzi, stop cosseting me! I'll manage. Now help me pack, sweetheart, and then we'll have a nice supper together. What time are you on duty tomorrow?'

Lizzi stopped fighting. 'Eight. When are you coming back?'

'Monday night, and give your old mother a hug!'

Lizzi bent down and wrapped her mother's fragile frame in her arms. 'I love you, Mum,' she said shakily.

She helped her pack, and then they spent a quiet evening together before having an early night. In the morning Lizzi helped her mother get ready, packed the last-minute things and put the case by the door.

'Ring me,' she said firmly, and left for work, still dubious but resigned.

When she got back that night the house was silent, truly empty for the first time in seven years. Her mother wasn't coming back during the evening, and Lizzi would be alone for the next few days. The evening dragged, and several times she looked at the phone, willing Ross to ring her. She almost rang him—anything to break the monotony—but she thought better of it and went to bed.

Friday was better, as she was working a split shift and wouldn't have the endless evening to deal with. She spent the afternoon at the shops, choosing a new dress for Ross's party on Saturday night, and finally settled on a soft silk jersey dress in a faded hyacinth-blue that exactly matched her eyes and made them seem enormous. She chose it for the colour alone, not really paying much attention to the style. With her tall, slender figure most things looked good on her, so after a cursory glance at the fit she bought the dress and a cream teddy in a lovely soft stretchy satin fabric to wear underneath it, and ran back to the hospital with minutes to spare.

As she arrived back on the ward, Ross appeared as if by magic and ushered her into her office. 'Hi,' he murmured, and gave her a quick hug.

'Hi, yourself. I haven't seen you since Wednesday. What have you been doing?'

He grinned. 'I've been around, but I've been dashing here and there. I got the car back, and I've moved out of residence at last. The removal men came yesterday with all my stuff, and I've been sorting through it.'

'How does the house look?'

He laughed. 'Chaotic! There's so much to do, but I'm not on duty tomorrow, and Oliver's registrar is covering Saturday night.'

'What about Mitch?'

'What about him? He's still smarting from the dressing-down I gave him on Wednesday. I invited him, and I don't know what he's more frightened of—coming, or staying away! How is Mrs Turner, by the way?'

'Improving. Her bowel sounds are returning, and we've removed the flatus tube. Her gastric juices are right down now, and she's maintaining her fluid balance nicely.'

'Excellent. I think we can stop aspirating now and try her on water, twenty mls two-hourly, and see how we go from there.' He levered himself off the edge of the desk and tipped her chin up with a long finger, somehow managing to turn the simple gesture into a bone-melting caress. 'When are you coming over tomorrow?'

She tried to ignore the shivers running up and down her spine. Heavens, it was only one finger on her chin! What was wrong with her? Somehow she found her voice. 'As early as you like. My mother's gone away for the weekend, so I can come round at nine, if you like.'

'I like. I'm off again. I'll see you tomorrow.' His mouth swooped down and brushed hers briefly, and then he was gone again, leaving her senses rioting.

She sighed. Ever since she'd met him she'd been on an emotional see-saw, and she found it desperately unsettling. Following on Ross's instructions, she went to remove the Ryle's tube from Mrs Turner and give her her first drink.

Amy Winship had made firm friends with the woman over the course of her setback, and Amy's confidence had increased a thousandfold as a result. Together they made Mrs Turner comfortable again, and then Lizzi called Amy into her office with her, shutting the door behind them.

'I gather the CNO had a word,' she began.

Amy nodded. 'She was hopping. I felt so dreadful about Mrs Avery, it was such a stupid thing to do and I can't imagine what possessed me, but I won't make the same mistake again! In fact, I can't afford to make *any* mistakes or the CNO says she'll have me out of nursing so fast my feet won't touch the ground!'

'I'm sure it would depend how serious the mistakes were. I remember when I first started nursing I washed all the thermometers in hot water and broke the lot—twenty-eight of them, if I remember correctly! That went down like a lead balloon, I can tell you! But I agree, you must be very careful to check if you're the slightest bit unsure about any procedure, because you literally have their lives in your hands. It's a huge responsibility, and it can be an awesome one.' She smiled reassuringly. 'You're coming on nicely, Amy. Just keep your head, and you'll be fine. How's Mrs Adams?'

'Oh, depressed, you know.'

'Yes, I do,' Lizzi said. 'I'll go and have a word with her. She's going home tomorrow, isn't she?'

'I wonder how she'll cope,' Amy said sadly. 'It must be dreadful. None of us have any idea what she's really going through, do we?'

Lizzi forced a smile through stiff lips. 'Don't make assumptions, Amy. Everyone has suffered something at some point in their lives. With a little compassion we can all understand, at least in some measure.'

Amy cocked her head on one side and looked at Lizzi thoughtfully. 'Have you ever been married or engaged, Sister?'

Lizzi opened her mouth to tell the girl it was none of her business, but for some reason the words wouldn't come out. 'Yes, I have,' she said quietly, 'so I do know, only too well, what Jennifer Adams is going through, and what she's got ahead of her. That's why I'm going to talk to her now.'

She left Amy looking slightly stunned, and let herself quietly into Jennifer Adams's little room. They had left her in the side-ward for privacy, and there were times when Lizzi wondered how wise a move it had been. Privacy, as she had found, was a two-edged sword, and too much time for thinking just threw you into a downward spiral. Lizzi knew, she'd been there.

She had had several conversations with Jennifer, but due to her own reluctance to let down her guard, and Jennifer's withdrawn state, they had been fairly brief and meaningless exchanges.

This, though, was different. Lizzi realised with horror that she was about to let down her guard, and she had to brace herself.

'Hello, Sister,' Jennifer said lifelessly.

'Hi.' The young woman was sitting on a chair, and Lizzi drew another one up beside her. 'How are you doing?'

She gave a half-hearted shrug. 'OK. I wake up, I get through the day, I go to bed and sometimes I sleep. I'll survive.'

'It gets easier,' Lizzi told her quietly. 'At first you think of nothing but your husband, every waking minute, and you'll wake up in the night and reach for him, and he won't be there. Then you'll get angry, after a while, and you'll hate all the things that took him away from you, like alcohol, young men, cars, the reason you were going out in the first place. You'll blame yourself—in your case you'll say that if you hadn't been driving, or if you hadn't stopped to put on the lipstick, or dawdled over dressing—the list is endless, and when you get to the end of it there's nothing left to hate, so you invent things and drag them round with you for a while. Then even that goes, and you'll find all that you're left with is emptiness.

'Even the greatest sorrow can't be kept alive for ever, and when it fades if you haven't made sure that you've got something there to fall back on you'll be left with nothing. That's dangerous, and you mustn't let it happen.'

Jennifer looked at her through tear-filled eyes. 'How did you know? That's just how I feel—how. . .?'

'My husband.' Lizzi let out a long, shaky breath. 'I was a little younger than you. We'd been married nearly a year, and David and I and my parents were all going out for dinner. It was my parents' wedding anniversary, but I had flu, so I stayed at home and they went without me. On the way home they were hit by a drunk driver, and David and my father were killed, my father with a broken neck, David with head injuries. My mother was left with badly damaged legs, and is unable to walk. We live together now.'

'How long did it take you to get over him?'

Lizzi met her eyes and shrugged helplessly. 'I don't know—years. I'm not sure that I really have yet. Maybe.'

'I heard two of the nurses talking yesterday about you and Mr Hamilton. They said you were seeing a lot of each other.'

'Oh. I. . .' Lizzi swallowed. 'It's nothing serious, but I think he'd like it to be.'

Jennifer closed her eyes. 'I don't think I could bear it if another man touched me. I love Peter so much—I can't believe he's gone!' Tears squeezed under her lids, and Lizzi put her arms round her and let her cry.

Strangely, this time she didn't feel anything other than compassion. Had Ross done so much for her? Had he really freed her from the prison of her grief? She realised with amazement that he probably had, but to what end?

So she could be hurt all over again?

She forced herself to concentrate on Jennifer, told her to get in touch with a bereavement counsellor whose name she gave her, and when she felt she could leave her again she went and did the drugs with Lucy Hallett and supervised the admission of a new patient.

By the time she got home, she felt worn out but somehow whole again. She had managed to do her job and be compassionate and human, without losing her authority. She shouldn't have been surprised, because goodness knew everybody else managed it, but somehow she was. Surprised and delighted. It was, after all, remarkably easy to be human!

* * *

Saturday dawned warm and sunny, with tiny fluffy clouds bobbing in the sky and shining peach in the early light. As the sun's rays warmed them, the clouds melted into nothing, leaving a wide expanse of cerulean blue. Lizzi bounced out of bed and headed for the shower, singing.

Yesterday's good feelings were still with her, and she was looking forward to Ross's party. That in itself was a surprise, because she normally steered clear of social gatherings, but this time was different—*she* was different, and she suddenly couldn't wait.

She drew up outside his house at a quarter to nine, and he answered the door dressed in nothing but a pair of old jeans. The curls on his chest were still damp, and his hair was standing on end where he had towelled it dry.

'Come on in,' he said with a grin. 'I've just had a swim. Magic! Make a cup of coffee and I'll be right with you.'

He bounded up the steps to the bedroom three at a time, and she headed for the kitchen, only to come to an abrupt halt as she entered it. You could hardly move for boxes! In the corner of the room, squeezed on the worktop cheek by jowl with a food processor and a box labelled, 'Private—Keep Out!' which was standing upside down, she found the kettle, the coffee-grounds and the coffee-maker.

By the time she had found two mugs he was back, his hair dried, his chest mercifully covered, and surrounded by the tantalising scent of cologne. She sniffed appreciatively.

'What, no pheromones?'

He grinned. 'You want pheromones, just hang around. By the time we've unpacked this lot and got the place ready for the party, there'll be plenty!'

He wrapped his fingers around one of the mugs and sniffed. 'Good, you found the real coffee.'

'Difficult not to. It's the only thing that isn't in a box! By the way,' she waved at the carton beside her, 'what's in that?'

He groaned. 'God knows! It's Callum's—I didn't enquire too closely! I'll put it in his room.'

He hefted the box into his arms. 'Come with me and have a look at the bedrooms.'

She followed him out, absently watching the smooth swing of his legs and the way his jeans clung lovingly to his neat bottom. It was a view she could grow very used to, she thought with a smile.

At the top of the stairs he turned and caught her watching him, and he chuckled at her confusion. 'Eyeing up the goods, sweetheart?' he said teasingly.

'You flatter yourself!' she retorted.

His grin broadened, and he lowered the box to the floor. 'Have I told you how intoxicatingly lovely you look today?'

'Oh, Ross!' Suddenly she felt breathless and feminine, and ducked her head to hide behind her hair. His strong, supple fingers threaded through the pale curtain and lifted it away, and, holding her still, he bent his head and kissed her.

With a ragged moan she slid her hands around his waist and pressed them against his spine. It was a mistake. Releasing her hair, he lifted her off her feet and carried her into his bedroom, dropping her in the middle of the vast, carved wooden bed.

'At last I've got you where I want you!' he said with theatrical evil, and she giggled and rolled away as he fell on her. He made a grab, but she rolled again, and plunged straight off the edge of the bed.

'Are you all right?' His worried face appeared above her, and she eased herself laughing to a sitting position.

'I think so.' She flexed her wrist tentatively, and he scooped her up and laid her—gently this time—in the middle of the bed.

'Sure? Want me to have a look?'

'It was my behind that came off worst,' she said foolishly.

'Roll over, I'll just make sure you haven't damaged it—ouch! What was that for?'

'Licentious behaviour. Kiss me better,' she said, and wondered in the next second what on earth had possessed her.

He paused, his face suddenly expressionless, and then he rolled away.

'I don't think so, angel. Not if we're going to get anything else done today.'

His voice was curiously strained, and while Lizzi grappled with rejection he stood up and went over to the window, running his hands through his hair and breathing hard.

'Ross?' she whispered. He turned slowly towards her, his eyes wary. 'Ross, what did I say?'

'Nothing. Forget it.'

'Ross, please! What did I do wrong?'

His hands clenched, and he stuffed them into his

pockets. 'Nothing wrong, exactly. Let's just sort one thing out for the record, though. How far were you about to let me go?'

'I thought—you were kissing me—how far did you want to go?'

He gave a short, humourless chuckle. 'Further than that. Come on, we've got lots to do. Are you really all right?'

She stood up slowly. God, how stupid could she get? At least he hadn't rejected her, although she must have been unbelievably naïve not to realise where things were going!

'I'm fine,' she said in a small voice.

His arms came round her and he brushed his lips against her brow. 'Good. I'm sorry if I upset you. I'm out of practice.'

Not as out of practice as me, Lizzi thought to herself. It was just so long since she'd romped with anyone—if ever! David hadn't been very demonstrative, and she couldn't remember ever having fun with him in the way she did with Ross. Perhaps she'd just forgotten, but she didn't think so.

But the fun was getting dangerous, too tempting, too—lord, too *intimate*! And she couldn't allow that. . .

She eased out of his arms. 'Good job I made that coffee. Come on, there's lots to do.'

They worked well together, unpacking china and glassware, loading and unloading the dishwasher over and over again until all the things were clean and put away in their respective slots.

By lunchtime they were hot, grimy and ready to stop.

'Swim,' Ross said, and Lizzi was too hot and bothered to argue.

She met him at the poolside, and together they swam a few lengths and then played in the shallow end, splashing and ducking and generally letting rip for a while until Ross called a halt and they trailed wetly in to get dried and return to the grind.

'You do realise,' she said as she met up with him in the hall again, 'that I haven't seen the sitting-room since it was finished?'

He smiled. 'Come on, then. But if you don't like it, be gentle with your opinion!'

He needn't have worried. She fell in love on the spot, and wandered round touching his pictures, his collection of jade and soapstone figures, his furniture; her fingers absorbed the colours and textures, the warmth, the diversity of the man that he was—the man she was growing to love. . .

She whirled away, her face an expressionless mask. 'It's wonderful,' she said brightly. 'Let's sort out the food for this evening, shall we?'

Ross shot her a puzzled look, but he followed her back into the kitchen and spent the rest of the afternoon following orders.

By six there was a bewildering array of bits and pieces—dips, cheeses, fruit, tempting little nibbles to be popped in the oven just before they were needed—and Lizzi was exhausted.

Ross stopped her by the simple expedient of catching hold of her hands and dragging her out of the kitchen.

'Enough,' he said firmly, and led her to the guest bedroom. 'I've put your things in here—have a bath and a rest, and then get ready. Nobody will be here until eight o'clock, and I don't want to see you until five to.'

It did seem a good idea. She decided to lie down for a few minutes to rest her aching feet, and snuggled down on the bed. It was soft but supportive, wonderfully comfortable, and it sapped all her resolve. Within seconds her eyes had drifted shut, and she was asleep.

She was awoken abruptly by a light tap on the door mere seconds later.

'Lizzi? Are you OK?'

'Of course I'm OK,' she said crossly.

'Just wondered. You're awfully quiet, love. It's nearly seven-fifteen.'

'What?' She shot bolt upright on the bed and eyed her watch in dismayed disbelief. 'Why did you let me sleep?' she wailed.

She heard his chuckle fading down the corridor as she headed for the en-suite bathroom. Instead of the long, lazy bath she had promised herself, she settled for a hasty shower, and then towel-dried her hair before tugging a comb through it and applying her make-up with as much care as she could muster at twice the speed of light.

Then she squirmed into the satin teddy, adjusted the straps and pulled on the dress. It fell softly around her waist and slithered down, settling with a tiny sigh just below the knee. Nothing too outrageous, she thought, and struggled to reach the zip.

'It's ten to eight. How are you doing?'

'OK. Can you give me a hand with this zip?' she said breathlessly, giving up her contortions and standing with her head bent and her hair held up off her nape with both hands.

The door opened and closed, and she felt his warm fingertips ease the zip up and then glide round the neckline, sending shivers down her spine.

She threw back her head and turned, and his eyes widened fractionally.

'Oh, Lizzi, you are spectacular!' A slow, sexy grin found its way from his eyes to one corner of his mouth, and her heart flipped and slithered in her chest.

'You don't look so bad yourself,' she murmured, still breathless but for quite a different reason. His silver-grey trousers were beautifully cut, subtly enhancing the sleek lines of his legs, and the shirt, soft muddy-green silk, fitted him to perfection. He was wearing a tie, a darker green with a tiny gold stud, and he looked wonderful.

She cleared her throat. 'Do you have a hairdrier?'

He nodded. 'In the bedroom on the floor. Help yourself. I just want to go and put the oven on and fill the ice-bucket.'

She slipped on her sandals and went into his room, located the hairdrier and carried it over to the ward-robe where there was a full-length mirror.

Her hair had started to dry, and, try as she might, it wouldn't lie sleekly but fell instead in a foaming mass of soft, wispy curls. It looked—wanton, she thought, and creased her brow. Oh, well, too bad. She put down the hairdrier and turned to have one last look—her first real look at the dress.

'Ye Gods!' she squeaked. 'Is it me?' It must be; the mouth in the mirror was moving at the same time. She closed her eyes, and opened them again slowly. No change. The dress slithered and shimmered and caressed and draped, at once revealing and yet mysterious, and wickedly, wickedly sexy.

'I can't wear it!' she wailed.

'Can't wear what?'

'This dress! Ross, it's obscene!'

He studied her seriously, and then lifted his eyes to her face. 'It's far from obscene, Lizzi. You look— beautiful. Absolutely lovely. Don't even think about changing.'

She turned back to the mirror, and closed her eyes. 'I can't!'

Just then the doorbell rang, and he took her hand firmly and led her with him down the steps to the front door.

'Ross, please!' she whispered frantically, but instead of releasing her so that she could go and panic in the bedroom he bent his head and kissed her until her senses were reeling.

Then, before she could recover, he opened the door.

'It's been a fabulous party, Ross,' she told him dreamily, hours later, as they strolled down the steps to the pool. Soft music followed them, and through the sitting-room windows above them they could see people dancing, others chatting and laughing, some unbelievably still eating little nibbles. It was getting hot inside, and a little wild, and they had slipped out for a bit of peace.

They weren't the only ones. One or two people were

wandering around the garden, and every now and then they heard the sound of soft laughter from the shadows.

He drew her into his arms. 'Dance with me,' he murmured, and pressed his hands gently against her spine, easing her up against him. Oh, he felt so good! He was whispering again, his voice husky in her ear.

'You've been driving me mad all evening in that dress,' he said. 'Do you know what I want to do to it? I want to slide the zip down, and ease it off your shoulders, and kiss every inch of you as I reveal it——'

'Every inch?' she whispered with a little laugh.

'Every single, delectable, pearly inch, until you're begging me to make love to you.'

Her legs felt weak with the thought. He wouldn't have to kiss many inches to persuade her tonight! She stumbled slightly against him, and giggled softly.

Was it the wine, or Ross's tempting voice that made her feel so wicked? Oh, what did it matter! She rested her head on his shoulder and smiled mischievously.

'Sounds wonderful,' she breathed. 'Do you know what I'm going to do to you?'

'Tell me,' he urged huskily.

'I'm going to put my hands on your chest like this——' she placed one each side over his ribs '—and push!'

With a startled yell he fell backwards—straight into the pool. She clutched her sides and laughed until she ached, by which time he had made his way to the shallow end and was striding up the steps, water streaming from him in all directions. He approached her steadily, a wicked gleam in his eye, and she suddenly wondered what she'd let herself in for.

'No, Ross,' she pleaded, backing away from him. 'Mind my dress, it cost a fortune.'

He was stripping in front of her, first his shirt—the tie was long gone—then the shoes and socks, then the trousers.

'Take it off, Lizzi,' he said conversationally.

'Don't be ridiculous!' she reasoned, and then squealed as he reached for her.

'Turn round and I'll get the zip.'

'Ross, no——'

'Do it, or you go in like that!'

She turned, frantically searching for an escape route. Perhaps if she scrambled up the table—his fingers coiled round her wrist, snagging her back against him. 'Thank you,' he said politely, and she felt the zip slide down and the fabric fall open.

He turned her, eased it off her shoulders, and caught it as it fell, hanging it out of harm's way on a chair. Like his tie, her shoes were long gone, and she stood before him clad only in the slinky satin teddy.

It was worth one last try. 'Please, Ross, I don't feel too good——'

He smiled, a predatory, wicked, happy smile.

'This will make you feel better.'

As she flew through the air, she caught a glimpse of a crowd of fascinated people standing at the top of the steps, cheering.

Then she hit the water.

CHAPTER EIGHT

IT WAS a golden opportunity, of course—Lizzi up to her neck in water, everybody else jumping in like lemmings—and the cartoonist had a field day.

> Legless Lizzi Takes The Plunge—Have We Only Seen The Tip Of The Iceberg? Is There More To Her Than Meets The Eye?

There followed a brief and apparently wholly factual account of the events leading up to the mayhem, which Lizzi had to take as gospel. Frankly, in the cold light of day she could remember very little of her outrageous behaviour.

After the first humiliating sortie into the coffee-lounge, she had retreated to her office, emerging only when strictly necessary for the performance of her duty. Each time, there was a great deal of nudging and grinning, which she pretended to ignore.

Halfway through the seemingly endless afternoon, just as she was taking two aspirin for her atrocious hangover, Ross strolled in looking thoroughly pleased with himself.

'How's the head?' he asked gently, trying to disguise his smile.

'Awful,' she moaned, and sank into her chair. 'Ross, how could you let me make such a complete fool of myself?'

This time he didn't try to hide the grin. 'Serve you right,' he said cheerfully. 'I thought you were having rather a lot of fun, and who am I to cramp your style?'

She wadded up a ball of paper and threw it at him, then moaned and propped her head on her hands. 'Pig!' she whispered. 'Have you seen the cartoon? I couldn't even bring myself to take it down! Where were you when I needed you?'

He smiled, that crazy, lop-sided, sexy smile, eased the cartoon out of his pocket and waggled it at her before returning it to the pocket. 'I think I'll keep this one myself. I don't trust you not to destroy it!'

He walked over to her and perched on the edge of her desk, tugging her against him. She rested her aching head against his side and exhaled softly. 'Never again,' she muttered.

'You're not a drinker, are you, Lizzi, love?'

'No, and I'm never going to be! I had two glasses of wine—two!—and one glass of that fruity punch.'

'Ah! *That* punch! I think someone doctored it, so to speak. I had one sip and warned the drivers to avoid it. I didn't think to warn you—sorry, sweetheart.'

'Don't sweetheart me! I want to die!'

He chuckled and rubbed her cheek gently. 'You'll live, darling. Come round the ward with me?'

She groaned and sat up straight. 'Do I have to?'

'Yes.'

She sighed and stood up. 'All right, but wipe that grin off your face or I'll be tempted to smack it!'

They were followed by a chorus of speculative whispers, innuendoes and knowing smiles.

After it was over Ross escorted her back into her

office and grinned. 'There, that wasn't too bad, was it?'

'Are you blind and deaf? It was awful! I'm never going to be able to raise my head out there again!'

'Don't over-react,' he said soothingly. 'I'll see you tomorrow,' and, with a quick kiss, he left her.

She only realised much, much later that at some point in the proceedings he had called her darling.

Monday was better only because the novelty had worn off and everyone else had forgotten about the party— more or less! As for Lizzi, she had decided that it was patently absurd to skulk around on her own ward, so she had got out the superglue and re-applied her old image.

It failed. Amy Winship smiled warmly at her and said hello; Lucy Hallett, who had been at the party with Mitch Baker, asked her advice about going to stay with his parents; and of course the other consultants, notably Jesus Marumba and Oliver Henderson, ragged her to bits.

Only Mitch was silent, but his knowing smile haunted her. She was more than ever sure that his was the hand responsible for her downfall, but there seemed no way to find out.

Ross popped in and out, but she wasn't going to see him that evening as the boys were due to arrive with Ann and Andrew. When she came off duty at four she made her way home and cooked a casserole for herself and her mother, not knowing what time they would get back from the painting weekend.

In the event her mother was returned by Edward

Blake at six o'clock, and she just had time to register a
tall, distinguished-looking man with greying hair and
twinkling eyes before he rushed off to drop the others
at home.

'You'll meet him properly later, darling,' her mother
said. 'He's taking me out for dinner.'

Lizzi was stopped in her tracks.

'Dinner?'

'Mmm. We'll go to that pub on the river again——'

'Again?'

'Oh, yes. We've done it before, it's nothing
new——'

'It's new to me! I had no idea you were going out
with him!'

Her mother smiled a smile of great contentment.
'He's been asking me for some time, but just recently
I've decided that it's silly not to go—and do you know,
it's been wonderful? We've had the most marvellous
weekend, so romantic!'

Lizzi's jaw dropped a little. 'Romantic?' she croaked.

'Mm-hmm. Terribly romantic. He's a lovely man,
Lizzi. I can't imagine why it took me so long to realise
it.'

Lizzi sat down hard.

'This sounds—serious, Mum.'

'Oh, it is.' Her mother looked at her fondly. 'I love
him, darling, and he loves me. He hasn't asked me to
marry me yet, but I have a feeling he will, and if he
does I'll accept.'

'But what about Dad?' Lizzi asked, shocked.

'What about him? He's dead, darling——'

'How could you forget him?'

Her mother's face clouded. 'Of course I haven't forgotten him. I loved him, and we built our whole lives around each other. I still miss him, and I probably always will. Loving Edward doesn't mean I have to stop loving your father, darling, but he's been gone for years, and I can't live in a vacuum for the rest of my life.'

'I'm sorry you feel like that,' Lizzi said quietly. 'I've done my best to make you happy and look after you——'

'Oh, darling! Of course you have—you've been wonderful to me, and I'll always be grateful, but there's been something vital missing from my life, and I've found it with Edward.'

'I can't believe it! It's too soon——'

'It's over seven years——'

'What does that mean? How *can* you have got over him? I haven't got over David, and you were with Dad far longer!'

'Are you sure you haven't got over David?' her mother asked gently.

Lizzi felt her body sag with misery. 'No. They said, if I just gave it time—but how much? How long?' she cried.

Mary's hand found Lizzi's and squeezed it understandingly. 'It takes more than time, you know. Time will take away the pain, but it takes love to drive away the emptiness and put happiness in its place. Believe me, I know. I felt just the same until I met Edward, but now—oh, Lizzi, I'm so happy with him. Suddenly my life has meaning again, and I can't tell you how wonderful that is!'

Lizzi blinked, hard, and gave her mother a desperate hug. 'I'm glad you're happy. I didn't mean to criticise. I hope it works out for you.'

'Thank you, darling.' Her mother's eyes were bright with unshed tears. Lizzi thought her own probably were, too. She cleared her throat.

'Tell me a bit about him.'

'Edward? He's wonderful—lots of fun, terrific sense of humour most of the time, but he's a stickler for punctuality—which reminds me——' Her mother glanced at her watch, and gasped in dismay. 'Is that the time? He'll be back in a minute, and I've still got to wash and change!'

'Want a hand?'

'Please, darling. I'd love a bath, if you could run it for me.'

Lizzi went into the bathroom and scrubbed at her eyes. Her mother, in love with someone else! She splashed her face with cold water, blew her nose and forced herself to get on.

By seven-thirty her mother was bathed, dressed, her make-up reapplied and waiting for Edward as the doorbell rang.

Lizzi went to open it, and he gave her a tentative smile. Good grief, she thought, he's nervous! She opened the door wider and returned his smile.

'Do come in. Mum's just got to put her coat on.'

'Thank you.' He followed Lizzi down the hall, and as they went into the sitting-room Lizzi turned to say something else to him and was stunned at the expression in his eyes.

'All set, Mary?'

His voice was like dark chocolate, and his smile was the smile of a lover. No, she thought, they can't be——!

But her mother's answering smile was every bit as warm and intimate, and Lizzi had the strangest feeling that she was intruding. . .

'Don't wait up for me, darling, I could be very late. I'll get myself to bed.'

'Are you sure?'

Her mother and Edward exchanged amused glances, and Mary patted her hand. 'I'm sure. I'll see you in the morning.'

Lizzi found herself superfluous as Edward took the wheelchair from her and steered it competently out of the door.

She closed the front door behind them, slithered down the wall and burst into tears.

Suddenly her mother didn't need her any more, and that was very hard to take.

When the first rush of tears had eased, she stood up stiffly and made her way to the kitchen. She didn't fancy the look of her supper any more—in fact, all she wanted to do was talk to Ross. She had an overwhelming, burning need to be with him, to tell him all about it and get his perspective on it.

Without stopping to think, she grabbed her coat and bag out of the hall cupboard, snatched up her keys and ran out of the door.

Her fingers were trembling as she fumbled for the ignition, and she had to force herself to calm down and take a few breaths before she could get the car working and get off the drive.

It seemed to take ages, but finally she arrived, pulling up beside a blue-grey Range Rover. She stared at it in confusion, and then remembered—Ann and Andrew were bringing the boys to Ross for the week, and she was absolutely the last person he needed turning up on his doorstep at this time!

Tears sprang to her eyes and she dashed them away, but they were immediately replaced by others, and in the end she gave up and let them fall.

She knew she had to get out of there, but she couldn't seem to find reverse. Grinding the gears again, she swore tearfully and dashed her hands across her cheeks. Machinery! It was never on her side!

Just as she found reverse, her door was opened and Ross leant in.

'Lizzi?'

She took her foot off the clutch and the car jerked backwards and stalled.

'Darling, are you all right?'

With a broken little cry she threw herself into his arms, and he crouched down and held her hard against his chest. 'Lizzi, what's the matter? Is it your mother? Tell me, love!'

'She's got a lover! Ross, I don't believe it! I had to talk to you——'

'Hush, love. It's OK. Come on in and have a drink and calm down.'

'You don't want me here! You've got your wife and children and——'

'My *ex*-wife, her husband and my sons would be delighted to meet you, and there's no way you're going anywhere until you've calmed down a bit, so come in like a good girl and let me look after you, eh?'

'Ross, I can't, I look an absolute wreck——'

'You look wonderful to me. Come on.' He took her hand firmly and led her out of the car and into the house. 'Go and freshen up. I'll wait for you in the kitchen.'

He gave her a little push, and she went up the steps to his bedroom and stared at herself in the mirror in his bathroom.

'Oh, my God!'

Amazing what a few tears and a little self-pity could do to the complexion, she thought dismally. She washed her face in cold water, patted it dry and re-applied her make-up with unsteady hands. She truly didn't want to meet Ann, especially not in these circumstances, turning herself inside out because her widowed mother had finally found happiness with someone else!

'Am I really so selfish?' she murmured miserably to herself. The answer had to be yes—why else had she got in such a state?

With a sigh, she made her way to the kitchen. Ross was thankfully alone, refilling glasses.

'There you are. I was just about to come and find you. What would you like to drink?'

'Nothing! I don't think I should have graduated off Ribena yet!'

He chuckled. 'Have some English apple juice.' He took a carton out of the fridge and poured some into a tall glass. 'Here.' He leant over and kissed her gently.

'You look fine now. Come and meet them. They're going soon and then we can talk.'

She closed her eyes, took a deep breath and followed him through the door and down the steps to the sitting room.

Then he turned to her and winked encouragingly. 'Lizzi, I'd like you to meet Ann and Andrew, and the boys—Callum, Alastair, come over here and be polite.'

She was aware of shaking hands with a diminutive, dumpy woman with twinkling eyes and a warm smile, and a tall man with thinning hair, and then she was facing his boys—Callum, nearly as tall as her and, barring a shock of dark hair, the image of his father, and Alastair, smaller, less bold, but still his father's son although the hair was fairer and the eyes were a bluer grey.

She smiled at the boys, and Alastair smiled back, his face accepting. Callum, on the other hand, regarded her warily for a second before turning away and slumping back on the settee.

Ross sighed. 'Ignore him,' he advised quietly, and ushered her towards his chair.

She wanted to run away, but she fought down the urge and sank gratefully into the soft leather, slipping off her shoes and tucking her feet under her bottom.

'You aren't allowed to put your feet up,' Callum said suddenly, and Lizzi blinked.

'Callum, *you* aren't allowed to put your feet up because you inevitably have muddy trainers on. Lizzi can do what the hell she likes, and, in any case, it's none of your damn business! Now apologise!'

'Leave him, Ross. He's just showing me my place in the pecking order,' she murmured.

'Well, then, he's mistaken!' he retorted. 'Apologise, Callum, or go to your room.'

The boy stood up and walked towards the steps, rebellion in every line of his body. 'God knows what she's doing here anyway. You don't usually let them over the threshold!'

Ross was across the room before Callum knew he was coming, and yanked him round to face Lizzi.

'Apologise!' he commanded, his voice deadly quiet.

The boy swallowed, obviously realising he had gone too far, and mumbled an apology, and then Ross marched him up the stairs in a stinging silence.

As their footsteps faded, Ann shrugged her shoulders in embarrassment and shook her head sorrowfully. 'Lizzi, I'm so sorry. He isn't usually so vile.'

Lizzi forced a smile. 'It's all right. I think I understand. I met my mother's new man friend tonight, and I could cheerfully have behaved like that!'

Alastair looked fascinated. 'Did he put his shoes up on the furniture?' he asked in awe.

She laughed, the humour of the situation hitting her suddenly. 'No, Alastair, he took her out to dinner, and I didn't appreciate it at all.'

Andrew chuckled, and Ann sighed with relief. 'I'm truly sorry about him. He is actually a nice boy.'

'I'm sure he is. It must be very difficult for him.'

'I don't think it's difficult for him at all,' Andrew said. 'He copes with me being married to his mother—why should his father be any different?'

'Perhaps because he's always had him to himself?

He's never had to share him with a woman before, and if he thinks he's going to have to I imagine he sees me as a threat to the status quo. Believe me, I understand that!'

Alastair grinned. 'I expect he was just surprised—you're much nicer than the brainless bimbo Dad ran around with in London——'

'Alastair! Not you, too!'

'Er—I wasn't—Dad, don't be cross!'

Ross shook his head in despair. 'Lizzi, I'm sorry. I don't know what's come over them.'

He crouched in front of her and took her hands. 'OK, sweetheart?'

'I'm fine. Did you kill him?'

'No. I was very careful—the bruises will hardly show in six months.'

She giggled, and he pressed her hands and stood up.

'Andrew, Alastair, come and give me a hand to bring in the luggage.'

'Yes, we ought to be off soon. Long day tomorrow.' Andrew unfolded his long legs and followed Ross out, and Alastair trailed after them, the picture of reluctance.

Finally Ann and Lizzi were alone—the past and the present, Lizzi thought. How bizarre.

Ann studied her quietly for a moment, and then smiled. 'Al's right, you know. You're much nicer than the brainless bimbo he ran around with in London for a while.' She ran her fingers thoughtfully along a seam in the chair, and then looked back at Lizzi, her gaze very frank. 'I've been worried about him,' she confided. 'He's been alone too long, and it's not good for him, but I know you will be. He's said so much about you, and I know he really cares for you.'

'He's a wonderful man,' Lizzi said quietly.

'I'm glad you think so. I always did.'

Lizzi's head snapped up. 'But you left him!'

'Because I didn't love him the way he deserved to be loved, and what I have with Andrew is so *right*! If I'd stayed with Ross, I would have cheated him, I would have cheated myself. We would have ended up hating each other, and that would have been a tragedy for the boys. As it is, we're good friends now and that's worth a lot. He was a good husband, you know. It was never any failing on his part that made me leave. I mean, he wasn't perfect, but he was always loyal, always there when he could be. He never went to the pub or played golf or did any of the things other men did. He took fatherhood very seriously—still does. That's my only real regret, that he missed the children growing up, but he's still a very attractive man, he could have another family. . .'

Lizzi met her searching gaze for a moment, but then her eyes fell and she stared sightlessly at her hands. Ross's children—her children—*their* children. . . Her heart pounded in her chest, and she felt an almost biological yearning deep in her pelvis. Oh, Ross! she thought achingly. Why did I have to meet you? Why did I have to fall in love? All that pain waiting to happen——

'All set, Annie, love?'

Lizzi dragged herself back to reality and stood up jerkily. Ann came over to her and took her hand, then kissed her cheek. 'Take care of him. He's one in a million.'

Lizzi shook her head helplessly, mumbled something incoherent and shook hands with Andrew.

She left them to say their goodbyes to the children in private. When Ross came back in she was standing at the shelves, stroking a fat little jade Buddha with her fingertips.

Ross's arms snaked round her waist and tugged her back against him. 'Seventeenth century. Note the carving on the base.'

Lizzi turned into his arms and buried her face into the curve of his shoulder.

'Tell me about it,' he murmured.

'It's—nothing, really. My mother's been taken out to dinner by a charming man, and I'm behaving very much like your thirteen-year-old son! Believe me, I can sympathise with him.'

'I can't. Evil-mannered wretch. I'm so sorry about his behaviour——'

'Forget it, Ross. I really do understand.'

He tugged her over to the settee and pulled her down beside him. 'Tell me about Mary and this fellow, then. How serious do you think they are?'

She laughed wryly. 'Oh, very. She thinks he's going to propose, and when he does, she's going to accept. I couldn't believe it——'

'I can. She's a very attractive woman, you know.'

'I realise that.' Lizzi's brow puckered in a frown. 'It's just—I thought it seemed a bit quick. I mean, I'm not ready yet——'

'Aren't you?' His gaze was guarded but intent, and

she had the strangest feeling that the answer mattered
to him more than he was letting on.

'No, I'm not. I didn't think she could be either, but
she said the strangest thing. She said it takes more than
time, it takes love. She said time takes away the pain,
but only love drives out the emptiness. . .'

Ross's gaze didn't waver. 'She's right, you know.
You should try it some time.'

She was held by his eyes, mesmerised, trapped by
the message they held, and then she was pulling away
from him, struggling to her feet, unable to get away
fast enough.

'I—I must go. I'm on an early tomorrow, and I could
do with a night's sleep, and you've got to sort the boys
out and get them unpacked and——'

'Lizzi?'

She stopped talking and headed for the door.

'Lizzi, wait!'

He followed her out, his footsteps firm and right
behind her. Just as she reached the car he turned her
round and pulled her into his arms, kissing her until
she was breathless.

'You won't run from me for ever. When you're
ready, I'll be here.'

She swallowed the panic that rose in her throat, and
letting herself into her car, she started the engine and
crashed into gear.

He opened the door and smiled. 'You really hate
that gear-box, don't you?' he said gently, and, with a
light kiss on her cheek, he shut the door and let her go.

All the way home his words echoed in her ears. 'You

won't run from me for ever. When you're ready, I'll be here. Won't run for ever—won't run for ever. . .'

'You want a bet?' she muttered as she slowed down for her drive, dredging up her determination. She was not going to let him persuade her—she wasn't!

Was she?

'No!' her mind screamed.

'Yes!' her heart pleaded.

She crashed the gears again.

CHAPTER NINE

OF COURSE, as luck would have it, Ross was the first person Lizzi saw that morning, and he seemed to haunt her elbow-room for the entire day.

She met him first of all as she was heading to her office for the hand-over from Jean Hobbs, when he leant too close and deliberately brushed against her as he opened the door.

'After you,' he said, his voice slithering down her spine like melted chocolate. She suppressed the shiver, and the urge to jam her elbow in his ribs, with equal vigour. One glance at his eyes was enough—he was in the mood to play, and Ross at play was Ross at his most dangerous as far as Lizzi was concerned.

For years she had been deprived of a playmate, someone with whom she could have fun and laugh about silly things, and she could feel her treacherous heart yearning towards him.

So she ignored him, avoided his wicked eyes and sat with her back to him.

It didn't stop the awareness, the tingling in her spine that told her he was watching her. As soon as she could, she despatched her staff to their routine tasks, detailed the necessary specials and organised the prepping of patients destined for Theatre.

Then she escaped, but he followed her, so close that when she turned round he bumped into her, catching her elbows to steady her and apologising with that rich, deep voice that made her heart lurch.

'You aren't in the least sorry,' she grumbled.

He twinkled at her.

'Shouldn't you be somewhere doing something useful?' she said crossly.

That wretched smile tipped his mouth and her heart went off at a tangent again.

'I want to talk to my list patients,' he said logically, and his smile broadened. 'Perhaps you could help me find them?'

Her lips tightened. 'You don't need me——'

'Oh, but I do! Just here and now is a little public, but if you give me a minute I'm sure we could arrange a time and a place——'

'Mr Hamilton!' She stepped back, conscious of the interested stares of her nursing staff, and wheeled round. 'Come on, then,' she snapped impatiently. 'If you want to see them, let's for goodness' sake go and see them!'

He fell into step beside her. 'Sister Lovejoy, has anyone ever told you you've got a shocking temper?'

'You could die young,' she hissed.

'No chance! I'm already thirty-eight, you've missed the boat. Now Callum—he could die young!'

She stopped and turned to him. 'You didn't take him apart because of me, did you? Ross, I saw his eyes— he was so resentful, so vulnerable—he looked almost frightened. I hope you didn't get too heavy.'

He sighed. 'No, not really. I gave him hell for being rude, but later on we had a chat—I think you're right, he's worried there'll be no place for him in my life. I told him there was no chance of that.'

Lizzi's heart stopped and then started again, and she was stunned at the shocking sense of disappointment that surged through her. Gracious, she didn't want to marry him, so why should it hurt so that he'd told his son there was no chance?

There was nothing like being told you couldn't have something to make you want it, she thought with irony. 'I—I'm glad you straightened him out,' she said, and to her astonishment her voice sounded almost normal.

They went round the ward, chatting for a few moments to each of the patients on Ross's list, and then he went up to Theatre to get ready and she went to prepare Mr Widlake for discharge.

He had progessed well, but an infection in the wound had held him back a few days. However he was now well on the way to recovery, and Lizzi would be sorry to see him go. He was a nice man, always friendly, never demanding, and she wished all her patients were like him.

Mrs Turner, too, whose paralytic ileus had brought Ross's wrath down on Mitch Baker's head, was also going home, her health restored. Amy Winship's confidence had grown enormously due to her kindly attitude towards the young nurse, and Lizzi silently blessed her for it. Amy would be a good nurse in the end, but without Mrs Turner she might never have made it.

What with one thing and another it was a busy morning, with patients going up to Theatre and then returning from Recovery on half-hourly obs for a while until they stabilised, and Lizzi didn't have time for coffee on the ward, far less in the staff canteen.

She met Ross there at lunchtime, though, and they talked about the boys and their schooling and Ross's concern that they should always feel they had a place with him, no matter what.

Why have I been worrying myself? she thought. Ross obviously had no intention of upsetting the status quo in his fragile family infrastructure, and here she was getting all worked up because he might want to marry her! Idiot! He wanted an affair, that much was blatantly obvious, but marriage? No way.

She was depressed.

They gravitated to the coffee-lounge and joined Oliver and Bron.

'Seen the board?'

'What?' Lizzi moaned.

'Oh, nothing nasty,' Bron hastened to reassure them, seeing Lizzi's long face. 'Just a joke—what happens when yetis sunbathe?'

They groaned in unison.

'They turn into baked Alaska.'

Lizzi giggled in spite of herself, and then sighed. How true. All warm and gooey on the outside, and still cold in the middle. Was Ross like that? Had she failed to reach him, except on the most superficial level? And why was she worrying about it? She didn't even *want* him!

She tripped over him for the rest of the day and tried to put her errant thoughts on hold.

Wednesday was no better, and on Thursday Ross

was off, taking the boys out for the day, and perversely she missed him.

On Friday she was faced with a dilemma. He asked her to spend Saturday with them, and she declined. 'I'm taking my mother shopping,' she explained.

'Dinner, then?' he persisted. 'If you don't, Callum will think it's his fault, and he'll have a massive attack of guilt.'

Lizzi relented. 'All right. I'll have dinner with you all.'

Saturday dawned bright and clear. She was pleased that they would have lovely weather. They were going to Cambridge, punting on the river, and good weather was an imperative.

She also tried to be pleased for her mother, who was going to an outdoor exhibition and craft fair with Edward, but just seeing them together brought on all sorts of peculiar emotions she didn't care to analyse, and that made dispassionate behaviour difficult.

At seven o'clock she dressed carefully but casually in soft print cotton trousers and a simple white blouse, with a cotton sweater thrown over the shoulders and knotted at the front, just in case it got cooler in the evening. As an afterthought she packed her swimsuit and a towel in a bag, and then left.

There was no answer to the doorbell, and trying the handle she found the door unlocked. As soon as she was in the hall she saw the reason.

Ross and the boys were playing water polo, and for a moment she stood still and enjoyed the sight of his body leaping and reaching for the ball, then she ran up to his bedroom and slipped on her suit.

She made it down to the pool without detection, and the first they knew of her presence was when she dived in and pinched the ball.

'Cheat!' Ross roared, and dived towards her. She held the ball above her head, and he surged up to her, reaching over her and bringing their bodies into intimate contact.

Their legs tangled, and his arm dropped in surprise.

'Hi,' he murmured, and his lips came down and brushed gently over hers.

'Hi,' she breathed, and lobbed the ball over his head.

'I knew you were a cheat!' he said calmly, and his arms slid around her. 'Cheats get punished.'

And with that he pulled her under the water and kissed her soundly.

By the time they came up for air they were both gasping, and their hearts were pounding nineteen to the dozen.

'Flirt,' she teased, and swam away from him, trying to ignore the delicious shivers running through her.

'Hello, boys.'

'Hi.' Callum threw her the ball. 'Want to join in?'

She smiled slowly at him. 'Thank you, Callum. Yes, I think I will.'

Lizzi sided with the boys against Ross, who complained that he was hopelessly outnumbered and yet still managed to do better than the other three put together.

After an outrageous few minutes when everybody broke or changed the rules whenever possible, they all made their way out of the water and into the house.

'Boys, dry your feet before you go in,' he reminded, and she grinned impishly.

'What about the girls?'

'The girls get their feet dried for them,' he replied, and his eyes held a promise. 'We have unfinished business, lady,' he murmured as he knelt by her feet. He dropped a kiss on to her instep and she sucked in her breath hard. What was he trying to do to her?

The boys were long gone, their towels dropped on the patio. She bent to pick them up, and took them into the kitchen.

'Where do these go?'

'Tumble-drier. Would you like a drink before you go and get respectable, or are you going to stay like that all evening with your pert little nipples jutting against that fabric and driving me wild?'

She dragged the towel up over her body and flushed scarlet, heading for the bedroom. He laughed softly at her retreat.

Once respectable again, she went back to the kitchen. 'Anything I can do?'

He glanced at her. 'Very pretty. Yes, you can decorate the kitchen—sit there, have a drink and tell me all about yourself. Do you come here often?'

She laughed, perched on the seat and accepted a weak gin and tonic.

'Remember I'm driving home later,' she told him.

'Oh, yes. What a shame. Sure I can't change your mind?'

She smiled slowly at his teasing expression. 'What would you do if I said yes?'

His smile faded, replaced by a look of startling

intensity. 'Curse, I expect. Still, the boys go back tomorrow. Why, are you about to?'

'No.'

'That's what I thought,' he said with an exaggerated sigh, and grinned again. 'In that case, I'll go and throw some clothes on.'

The evening went well, except that Alastair began to feel a little queasy at about nine and went reluctantly to bed.

Callum followed shortly, leaving Ross and Lizzi alone.

'Mmm,' he said with a sigh, and slid down in his chair with his feet up.

'Are you quite comfortable?'

'Uh-huh. Eaten too much, but that's my fault.'

Lizzi's brow puckered in a frown. 'You didn't eat that much. I've seen you put away far more.'

He shrugged. 'Just didn't feel hungry, really. Probably all the pool water I swallowed when the boys mobbed me.'

'I expect you deserved it,' she said drily.

Just then Callum appeared at the top of the steps. 'Dad, Ally's been sick.'

Ross closed his eyes and groaned. 'Just what I need.'

'And I feel sick too, now.'

He opened his eyes and studied his son's pale, clammy face with a resigned expression.

'Go and lie down, Cal. I'll deal with Alastair.'

He pried himself out of the chair, and swayed.

'Ross, are you all right?' Lizzi asked, worried.

He shook his head gently as if to clear it, and took

her proferred arm. 'Not really. I feel as sick as a parrot and incredibly dizzy.'

'Bed,' she told him, and steered him up the steps. When they reached his room, she propped him up, stripped off his jeans and jumper and pushed him gently on to the bed.

She found Alastair kneeling on the bathroom floor hanging over the loo, and stayed with him for a while before washing his face and hands and wheeling him back to bed, only to return to the bathroom moments later with Callum for a repeat performance.

She heard Ross stumble out of bed and slam his bathroom door, and rolled her eyes. It was going to be a long night.

By two o'clock the boys had settled and were asleep, exhausted. She had found some sachets of Dioralyte and mixed them up with water, and they had tolerated the electrolyte solution fairly well. In fact it seemed to help stabilise them, and once they had stopped vomiting she changed their sheets and they fell asleep almost immediately.

Ross, however, was a different story. He didn't want her near him, which she could understand, but she told him not to lock the bathroom door. He grumbled, but after one particularly loud thump she went in to find him crashed out full length on the floor, out for the count.

He came to almost immediately, doubled up and clutching his abdomen, and his whole body was suddenly drenched with sweat.

'I want to die,' he groaned, and she smiled grimly and helped him to his feet.

'Here or bed?' she asked.

'Here—go away!' he croaked.

She left him to it, taking the opportunity to change the sheets and mix him some Dioralyte.

When she heard him moving around again she went and prised him off the bathroom wall and helped him back to bed, arguing all the way.

'I want a wash——'

'I'll wash you; get into bed before you fall over again.'

'Don't treat me like a baby,' he said with as much firmness as he could muster, but it came out like the protest of a petulant child and she treated him as such.

Once he was talked back into bed, she brought the bowl she had used to wash down the boys and filled it with warm water, then washed him gently but thoroughly.

'That could be addictive,' he whispered hoarsely as she blotted his limbs dry, and tried for a grin. 'Perhaps I'll have a second childhood?'

'I thought you already were. Have you got any pyjamas?'

He cranked up an eyebrow. 'Pyjamas? Don't be ridiculous. What would I do with pyjamas?'

'Wear them in bed,' she suggested drily, and rummaged through his drawers until she found some clean pants.

'Here, put these on.'

She left him to change while she emptied the bowl, and then found him with one leg in and one leg out, collapsed against the side of the bed.

'I fell over,' he said with an apologetic smile.

She hoiked him back into bed, finished the job and covered him up.

'Drink this,' she coaxed, holding out the Dioralyte.

He pushed it away. 'Yuck.'

'Ross, please try it—you need to replace your electrolytes and keep your fluids up.'

'That'll certainly get my fluids up!' he said with a weak attempt at humour, and then fell asleep, propped up against the pillows.

With a sigh Lizzi eased him down the bed, straightened the pillows and looked longingly at the space beside him.

Just for a moment, she promised herself, and lay down, her hand resting on his shoulder, asleep as her head hit the pillow.

She was woken at five by Ross, groaning and thrashing from side to side.

Propping herself up on one elbow, she leant over him and rested her hand on his brow. He didn't seem to have a temperature, but he was very sticky and obviously in pain.

She watched as his eyes opened, and he groaned again and stumbled out of the bed.

When he came back, he was grey and shaking, and she washed him down again and tucked him up, just to watch him rush off once more moments later.

'I think my guts are going to rupture,' he croaked pitifully after about an hour. 'Never again will I dismiss anyone who says they've got abdominal pain—believe me, it hurts!'

Lizzi checked the boys but both were sleeping peacefully. So why was Ross so bad?

'What did you have for lunch?' she asked him the next time he woke.

'Beefburgers,' he said faintly. 'I had two, the boys just had one because they had chips.'

'That could be why you're so much worse.'

He roused himself to ask how they were, and allowed Lizzi to chivvy him into a drink of Dioralyte.

After that he seemed to settle for a while, and by eight o'clock he was heavily asleep for the first time.

Lizzi rang her mother to explain the situation, and then went to lie down in the guest room. She didn't want the boys catching her curled up with Ross and coming to any wrong conclusions!

They were up by ten, and like healthy puppies they were fit and raring to go. Lizzi found it incredible that they were asking for breakfast, but she made them toast and tea and forbade them to have a fry-up.

'Think of your father,' she admonished gently. 'How would he feel with all those greasy smells drifting through the house?' A thought occurred to her, and she frowned. 'Boys, what time do you have to be back at school?'

'Four,' Callum replied through a mouthful of toast.

'You ought to leave at three, then, at the latest—I don't think your father's going to be up to it by then. Do you know the way?'

They nodded. 'We can show you on the map, and once we're nearly there we can find it easily. Only thing is, we've got scads of junk—will it fit in your car?'

'Oh. No, probably not. Well, I dare say it can be sent on——'

'Take mine.'

'Ross! What are you doing out of bed?'

'Feeling bloody awful. How are you, boys?'

They eyed him thoughtfully.

'Fine,' Callum said.

'Better than you,' Alastair added, and went and hugged him gently.

He did look dreadful. His eyes were sunken and smudged, his face deathly pale, and even overnight he seemed to have lost weight. His hand came up and ruffled Alastair's hair, and he sagged against the doorframe.

'Bed,' Lizzi said firmly, and, tucking herself into his armpit, she grabbed his wrist as it dangled over her shoulder and wheeled him back to his room.

He sank back against the pillows with a huge sigh of relief. 'God, I feel as weak as a kitten. Do you mind taking the boys back?'

'Of course not—why do you think I offered?'

'Heroism?'

She grinned. 'Wrong sex.'

He grinned back. 'I had noticed,' he told her with a weary twinkle.

'Humph! You're getting better!'

'You don't have to sound so disappointed!' he said with a sigh, and slumped down the bed. 'I could murder a cup of tea.'

'Have your symptoms—er—subsided?'

He cranked an eye open. 'You are so delicate. Yes, my symptoms have—er—subsided, thank you. I just feel as if I've been ten rounds with King Kong.'

She smiled cheekily. 'You look it, too. I'll get you some tea, then I want you to go back to sleep.'

'Bossy,' he mumbled, but his eyes were already drifting shut. She didn't bother with the tea, instead waiting for him to wake again.

By a quarter to three he was looking much more human but still not well enough to drive the car, so she set off with the boys and left him lying on the settee watching a terrible old film on the television.

At first she was nervous driving the car—it was so much bigger than hers, and everything seemed to be electric or power-assisted. After treading on the brakes and nearly snubbing her nose on the steering-wheel, she learnt to use a little subtlety, and she discovered quickly that the accelerator worked with similar enthusiasm.

The boys didn't seem worried, though, and gradually she relaxed and allowed herself to enjoy it. As they drew nearer to the school, Callum leant forward and tapped her on the shoulder.

'Lizzi? Thanks for looking after us all last night.'

'You're welcome,' she smiled.

'Really? After the way I spoke to you?'

She heaved a sigh. 'Yes, even so. I don't suppose you really meant it, and, anyway, I did understand. Callum, you don't have to worry about me. I'm not a threat, you know. Your father and I aren't going to be married.'

There was a potent silence for a moment, and then Callum cleared his throat. 'Er—we wouldn't mind—I mean, you seem to be good for him, and he's very lonely—we can't be here all the time, and when we aren't it must be very quiet—don't you love him?'

Oh, God! She swallowed. It was like tiptoeing through a minefield blindfolded and wearing snowshoes!

'Your father and I are very fond of each other,' she began cautiously.

'He loves you, you know,' Callum told her bluntly. 'He said so.'

'Did he indeed?' she said, her heart pounding. 'Well, he hasn't told me that——'

'Are you having an affair just for kicks, then?'

'Ally! You can't ask her that!' Callum exclaimed, scandalised.

If Lizzi hadn't been so shocked, she would have laughed.

'Actually, boys, I hate to disillusion you, but your father and I aren't having an affair—and if we were it wouldn't really be any of your business.'

Teenagers! she thought, and waited in suspense for the next volley.

'We wouldn't mind, you know,' Callum put in.

'Well, thank you, boys. I'll tell your father we have your permission and see what he says, shall I?' she said drily. 'Now, where's this school?'

She was astonished when, having unloaded all their stuff at their boarding-house, they turned to her and hugged her. She hugged them back, hard, and watched as they went in, waving goodbye as they went through the door.

There was a silly lump in her throat. They were nice boys, for all their impudence, and she felt strangely bereft to know that she wouldn't be a part of their lives in the future.

Had Ross really told them that he loved her? But he'd said he'd told them there was no chance of him getting married again—so what had he really said? And what was he up to? It was time to find out.

He was still on the settee when she got back, but he was fast asleep, his lashes absurdly long and dark against his pale cheeks. He looked innocent and vulnerable, and she had an overwhelming urge to hug him. His silver hair was rumpled and falling over his brows, and she perched on the edge of the settee and smoothed it back. His eyebrows twitched together into a little frown, and his lashes fluttered.

'Lizzi?' he murmured.

'Who else? Are you OK?'

'Mmm. Boys back all right?'

'Yes. Have you had anything to drink?'

'Nag, nag, nag!' he grumbled gently, shifting on to his back and stretching. His shirt pulled out of his jeans, showing a narrow strip of hair-scattered middle that made her body clench with desire.

Ridiculous, considering that he had been dashing about half the night in just a pair of skinny briefs, and sometimes not even that, and she hadn't turned a hair! Her fingers itched to touch him, to feel that strip of skin and see if it was as soft, as satin-smooth as it looked beneath the fine curls.

She swallowed convulsively, and he chuckled.

'Go ahead, touch me,' he murmured.

'What?' she croaked.

'Touch me, Lizzi.'

She stood up and crossed to the window.

'Why on earth should I want to do that?'

'Because you want me? Because I want you? Search me. Maybe because it's time we stopped avoiding this and faced it head-on.'

She hugged herself with her arms and turned to look at him. 'I didn't think there was anything to face,' she said quietly.

'What?' His brows furrowed in a frown, and she shrugged helplessly.

'Is there? Anything to face?'

He stood up slowly and tucked his shirt back into his jeans. 'I thought so.' He ran his hands through his hair, and then stuffed them into his back pockets—to keep from strangling her, she thought. He certainly looked as if he was about to get mad.

'Callum said you loved me.'

His head snapped up, and he fixed her with a penetrating stare. 'How did that crop up?'

She laughed, a forced, rather shrill little sound that cut off abruptly. 'He thought you ought to get married, I think. Silly child.'

'He isn't a silly child. I happen to agree with him——'

'What? But you said you'd told him there was no chance!'

'When did I say that?'

'Oh, lord—after he was rude to me—Tuesday, I suppose. You said he was worried that you'd get married and there'd be no place for him, and you'd told him——'

'That there was no chance that there'd be no place for him, not that I wouldn't get married again.'

Her jaw dropped, and she turned away, trying to come to terms with what he had said.

'You're looking confused.'

'I—I am. I thought—oh, hell!' She paced across to the other window. 'I thought you wanted an affair——'

'No. No, I don't want an affair. I told you before, I want everything, your mind, your heart, your body, all of you. I love you, Lizzi. I've tried to give you time, give you space to get used to the idea, but I need you, love—I need you now.'

'Oh, God, no!' she whispered, her heart pounding. His voice was husky with emotion, his eyes like hot coals, glowing with passion, with raw, urgent need.

'Yes.'

'But——' Her lips were dry, and she ran her tongue round them. Ross's eyes narrowed and his body stiffened, as if he was holding himself back. She looked away. 'I need time——'

'You keep telling me that. How much time, Lizzi, love?' His voice was racked with pain. 'How much bloody time do you need? A week? A year? A lifetime?'

She gave a choked little cry and pressed her hand to her mouth.

'Don't push me——'

'Why?' He was much closer now, so close that she could feel the heat from his body. 'Why can't I push you?'

'It isn't fair——'

'You think what you're doing to me is fair? Damn it, Lizzi, I love you! Doesn't that mean anything to you?'

'Don't!' she cried softly, her voice a thread of anguish. 'I never wanted to hurt you, Ross, but I'm so afraid!'

Instantly his arms were around her, cradling her against his chest.

'Don't be afraid—I'll be here for you. I'll never hurt you——'

His lips came down and captured hers, and her body leant into his and clung helplessly as he plundered her mouth.

His lips trailed down to her throat, pressing hot, open-mouthed kisses over her heated skin.

'I love you,' he murmured, and she felt her heart shatter.

'Ross, no!' she sobbed, and something of her desperation must have reached him because he let her go, lifting his head and gazing down at her with pain-filled eyes.

'Why? Why are you so afraid?'

A tear slid down her cheek, and his thumb traced its path with great tenderness.

'If I stay—if I let you love me—when you go, I'll fall apart. I couldn't stand it all over again.'

'I'm not going anywhere, darling.'

'You could—you could leave me, like Ann left you, or—or like David. . .'

Her voice trailed into nothing, and he watched her as she shrugged helplessly.

'So that's it.' He gave a shaky sigh. 'Let me get this straight. Are you saying you'll deny us both the possibility of years of happiness just on the off-chance that one of us might die?'

'It's not an off-chance! It happens! It happened to me, it happened to my mother, and it happened to Jennifer Adams. Believe me, Ross, that is not an off-chance!'

'What about the chance that we could be happy? That's much more likely, and yet you're prepared to forgo it out of sheer cowardice!'

'It's not cowardice!' she denied. 'Ross, you don't know how it feels——'

'I can imagine. I can't guarantee you forever, Lizzi, I know that. I wish I could. All I can say is that as long as I live I will be there for you, and I'll do everything in my power to make you happy. I can't promise to live forever, any more than you can, but I'll do my utmost to make you happy as long as I'm alive.'

Her eyes flooded with tears. 'Ross, I can't take the risk!' she whispered. 'If I stop this now, it'll be bad enough, but if I let you—if I stay—I can't! I'm sorry— so sorry. . .'

His jaw clenched, and he bit his lip.

'Just tell me one thing. Tell me—tell me that you don't love me.'

'I—I can't!' she mouthed.

He took a shuddering breath, and his eyes closed. A single, heavy tear squeezed from under his lashes and slipped slowly down his cheek.

She reached out a hand and laid it on his chest; it shook and heaved beneath her palm.

'Just—go, if you must,' he whispered brokenly, and with one last, anguished look at his ravaged face she fled past him and out of his life.

CHAPTER TEN

LIZZI couldn't remember ever feeling so totally, devastatingly, mind-blowingly miserable in her entire life. When David had died, she had been cushioned by shock, and the necessity of keeping her mother going in the face of her bereavement and extensive injuries had to a certain extent prevented her from dwelling too much on her own loss, at least at first. Then rage and guilt had taken over in equal proportions, and she had had a focus for her anger in the drunk driver who had been responsible.

Now, she had nothing to cushion her, and she felt as if every nerve-ending had been flayed raw.

Her throat ached, her head pounded, she couldn't eat or sleep, and her already slender frame faded almost to nothing in days. She didn't notice—all she was aware of was Ross, polite, distant, absent whenever possible, moving quietly around the ward on his rounds, obviously subdued but making no attempt to change her mind.

He looked awful. He had dark shadows under his eyes, his cheeks were sunken and his normally laughing eyes were remote and cool—almost as if he wasn't there.

The staff, of course, noticed the yawning chasm that had opened up between them, and to a certain extent closed ranks. James Hardy, Ross's senior registrar, was distinctly cool towards her, and Amy Winship and Lucy Hallett were protective and motherly, almost to the point of making Lizzi want to scream. Lucy did the ward-rounds with Ross whenever possible, and Lizzi was only too grateful.

Breaks were the worst. The first day she had headed towards the usual group, only to pull up short when she saw Ross sitting with them. Their eyes had met, and with a lop-sided twist to his lips he had stood up, bowed slightly in her direction and walked away, his back ramrod straight. The others had been wary and tried to avoid any personal topic, sensitive to the appalling atmosphere, but it was agony nevertheless, and as the week wore on it got worse.

It came to a head on Thursday. It was a bad day from the beginning. On the way into the car park Ross and Lizzi had almost collided, and he gave her a grim little smile and waved her on with studied courtesy. She crashed the gears, predictably, and he laughed, a humourless little laugh that turned into a grimace. Their eyes tangled, and for once the shutters lifted and she saw the raw misery in his eyes.

Crashing the gears again, she drove to one end of the car park and he drove to the other. They met at the door, Ross slightly ahead of her, holding it open so she couldn't even hang back and let him go first.

Instead she hurried past him with a muttered 'Thank you,' and fled down the corridor.

He was operating in the morning, so she felt safe going into the canteen a little earlier than usual.

There was a crowd around the bulletin board, but there usually was, so she didn't pay a great deal of attention until she caught the curious glances thrown in her direction.

None of the normal group were there this early, so she was sitting alone and trying to ignore the pointed looks when Bron came in.

She glanced from Lizzi to the crowd around the board, and they melted away as she approached. Lizzi heard her indrawn breath, and rose unsteadily to her feet.

'Another one?' she said raggedly as she went over to the board. 'What's he dredged up now?'

Bron moved aside, her face reflecting her concern.

Lizzi's eyes widened as she took in the content of the cartoon. There was a vast bank of drawers like a huge wall of filing cabinets, and the middle one was hanging open; Ross was lying in it, his sword on his chest, while Lizzi pushed it shut with a victorious expression on her face.

The caption read,

Deep Freeze Is On! Ice Maiden Closes File On Yeti As A New Ice Age Commences!

With a choked cry, Lizzi whirled round and ran, almost bumping into Ross and Oliver as they came through the door together.

'Lizzi? What is it?'

She ran on, ignoring Ross's voice, down the corridor and out into the garden behind the nursing school. There she sank down on to a bench, heedless of the tears pouring down her face, and waited for the pain to go.

*   *   *

'I think the answer is on the board,' Oliver's voice murmured.

'What?' Ross dragged his attention back from Lizzi's retreating figure and turned to face his colleague.

'Over there.'

The usual cluster was beginning to form around the board again, but they faded into the woodwork as Ross's furious stride took him across the room.

'Bastard!' he hissed, taking in at a glance the significance of the drawers. Wrenching out the drawing-pins, he yanked the picture off the board and strode towards the door, barging into Sir Stephen Barrimore, Professor of Physical Medicine and chairman of the medical board, as he came in.

'Ah, Mr Hamilton! I've been meaning to have a word with you——'

Ross contained his temper with difficulty. He was breathing fast through his nose, his teeth clenched, and Sir Stephen's eyebrows climbed majestically up his craggy forehead.

'Something upset you, dear boy?'

Ross thrust the cartoon at him.

'Oh, another one of those. I must say, they've been rather amusing—although this one seems in rather poor taste——'

Ross snatched it back. 'You could make yourself useful, *sir*, by finding this bastard before I do, or you may find you're one doctor short!'

The man tutted and adjusted his glasses on his bulbous nose. 'Rather extreme, dear boy, don't you think?'

Ross snorted. 'You didn't see Sister Lovejoy—if

you think my attitude's extreme, I suggest you have a look at her personnel file! A bank of mortuary drawers is not something she can be expected to find amusing!'

He pushed past the astonished professor, and ran down the corridor in the direction Lizzi had taken. Not being familiar with the hospital, he had no great hopes of being able to find her, and after a while he returned to the ward to discover that she was in her office.

'Where have you been?' she asked woodenly. 'They've been looking for you. You've got three patients prepped up——'

'Are you all right?'

She met his worried gaze with eyes blank with misery.

'Yes, I'm all right,' she whispered.

'I'll get him, Lizzi. I'll find out who it is and I'll get him.'

He turned on his heel and marched out of the room. She ran after him.

'Where are you going?'

'Theatre—give me two minutes.'

Lucy Hallett was at her elbow. 'Shall I send the next patient up?'

'Please.'

She went back into her office, closed the door and burst into tears.

It took him until lunchtime, but he caught up with the culprit in the end. He was coming from Recovery when he noticed one of the young surgeons scrubbing up. On the middle and index fingers of his right hand, he had a black inky stain.

'Gotcha,' Ross whispered to himself.

It was nearly two by the time Mitch Baker finished in Theatre and returned to his room in the residence, and Ross was waiting for him.

'About time,' he muttered tersely.

Mitch gave Ross a wary smile. 'Hello, sir. What can I do for you?'

'In here——' he indicated Mitch's room with a jerk of his head.

'Er—wouldn't you rather go to the bar? We can get a coffee——'

'In! What I have to say to you, believe me, you won't want to hear in public!'

Mitch opened his mouth and closed it again, and then unlocked the door.

There was a table under the window, and strewn across its surface were pens and pencils, bottles of Indian ink and scraps of cartridge paper, covered with little caricatures of Ross and Lizzi.

Ross kicked the door shut, and Mitch swallowed hard.

'Do you have any idea what you've done?' he raged.

'It was just a bit of fun, sir——'

'Fun? My God, you have a warped sense of humour!' He thrust the cartoon under Mitch's nose. 'What is that?'

He shrugged nervously. 'You in a freezer——'

'Correction—me in a refrigerated mortuary drawer!'

'So?'

'So? What do you mean, so?' He stood over Mitch, his finger jabbing him in the breastbone. 'I'll tell you, shall I? Lizzi Lovejoy—Mrs Lizzi Lovejoy, to be precise—is a widow! You couldn't have been more devastatingly accurate if you'd tried!'

Mitch's face was appalled. 'I had no idea—I'll apologise to her——'

'Damn right you'll apologise! Do you realise that in less than four weeks you've managed to fix a drain so insecurely that it fell out, give another patient paralytic ileus through your bungling incompetence, and now this! You do not have time to waste lampooning your superiors, Dr Baker, when your level of professional ability is so abysmally low! If you want to draw little pictures, I suggest you get an anatomy book and copy a few anatomical diagrams to bolster your insipid grip on your subject!'

He drew a deep breath and lowered his voice. 'I will be watching you, Dr Baker. You will be with me, operating beside me and under my tutelage, from now on. I don't care what anybody thinks, you are not an asset to the medical profession and until I'm satisfied that you know what you're doing you will be supervised in every professional moment, either by me or by James Hardy. Is that clear?'

Mitch nodded, totally humiliated.

'I want a written apology to Sister Lovejoy on her desk within the next fifteen minutes, and from now on you keep your damned interfering little nose out of her affairs. I don't care what you say about me, but you leave her severely alone—is that clear?'

He nodded again.

'I'll be in my office—I want to see you there as soon as you've delivered your apology—and if you get called to Theatre in the meantime, I want to know, because I'm going to be there. Understand?'

'Yes, sir.' He sighed heavily. 'About the cartoons—I'm sorry, sir. I didn't mean to hurt anyone. I didn't realise—she's always been cool and distant, but nobody knew why. I suppose we all thought she was just unfeeling. It never occurred to any of us that she had a reason for it. I'm not vindictive, sir. I wouldn't have done it if I'd realised.'

Ross gave a grim little laugh. 'You're not the only one who's made mistakes, Mitch,' he said wearily, and, with that enigmatic comment, he left the young registrar alone with his conscience.

Thank God she was on a half-day. As she let herself into the house, Lizzi's only thought was to make a cup of tea and retreat to her bedroom pleading a headache, but as she walked past the sitting-room she saw her mother and Edward through the open door, sitting together on the settee with their arms around each other, laughing and kissing and generally behaving like playful lovers.

She jerked to a halt, mesmerised, and her mother's head lifted at the sound of Lizzi's harshly indrawn breath.

'Hello, darling! You're home early!'

'Evidently!' she said with a brittle laugh.

Her mother's face registered disappointment, but Lizzi ignored it. Her emotions were too shredded to permit her to watch her mother kissing and cuddling with her lover in broad daylight.

'Did anyone ever tell you you're a prude?' Mary said gently.

Lizzi had the grace to blush. 'I'm sorry. It's been a rotten day. There was another cartoon——'

She broke off and turned away. 'Do you want a cup of tea?'

'Edward will get it. Come here, I've got something to tell you.'

She went in and perched on the edge of a chair— poised for flight, her mother thought—and smiled carefully.

'Fire away!'

'Edward has asked me to marry him, and I've said yes. Of course, I won't be living here any more, but you're welcome to the house—I'll get it transferred to your name, because I won't need it, and it'll be yours in the end anyway——'

Lizzi burst into tears and ran from the room. How could she talk about leaving the house to Lizzi in that matter-of-fact way? How could she marry Edward? How could she take the risk? 'What about me?' she sobbed, and threw herself down on her bed, her battered heart shaken by this new onslaught.

The bed dipped, and a warm, firm hand came down on her shoulder.

'Is it really such a tragedy that your mother could find happiness again?'

She sniffed and choked down the sobs.

'Go away,' she croaked.

'No. I want to talk to you. Your mother's very

worried about you, and so am I. Now sit up, blow your nose and drink this cup of tea while you listen to what I have to say.'

She did so, clearing her throat of the clogging tears and smiling sheepishly at him. 'I feel an idiot. I don't know what came over me——'

'You look bloody awful. What happened to the lovely, radiant girl of the last few weeks?'

Her face crumpled. 'He wants me to marry him. . .'

'And?'

'I can't!' she cried softly. 'I want to, I want to so much, but I just can't.'

'Why?'

She shook her head dumbly. 'I'm afraid.'

'Are you? Or are you feeling guilty because you're still alive and David isn't?'

Her head jerked up. 'No!'

'Sure? I've been through it, too, Lizzi. Think about it. If it's guilt, it's irrational. Of course his death was a tragedy, but your life has to go on, and living it in a kind of limbo is such a waste. Every day that you waste is gone, lost forever. You've only got one life, and you can't afford to squander it cn misplaced guilt!'

She drew in a sharp breath, and her hand flew to her chest, to steady her pounding heart. 'But I'm afraid to love again!'

'Correct me if I'm wrong, but don't you love him already? And isn't what you're feeling the very thing that you're afraid will happen? That you'll have to live without him and then your life will have no meaning? Lizzi, look at yourself! You're grieving for him, but he's still alive. He's out there, alive and well and loving you, and you're sitting here afraid to go and tell him how you feel!'

Her hand fell unnoticed to her lap. 'God, I've been such a fool! Of course I love him. It couldn't possibly feel any worse, no matter what—and here I am carrying on as if he's dead! Oh, Edward, thank you!'

She flung her arms around his neck and gave him a huge hug, then she bounced off the bed and ran back into the sitting-room.

'Oh, Mum, I'm sorry I was such a grouch! I didn't mean to be—it's just been a hell of a week, what with one thing and another. I hope you'll be very happy together.' She hugged her mother, gave her a big kiss and sank down on to the settee beside her. 'I'm going to see Ross, thanks to Edward, to try and sort this thing out. I think you're marrying the most sensible person I've ever met!' she said with a grin.

Mary and Edward exchanged relieved glances, and Mary patted her hand.

'I'm so glad you've come to your senses, darling. I've been so worried about you.'

'I'll be fine. I'll wait until he's home, and I'll go and see him. As for the house—hopefully I won't need it!'

She went back into her bedroom and paused at the dressing-table. From a silver frame, a cheerful stranger laughed up at her. With a gentle smile, she picked up the photograph and put it carefully into a drawer. Then with fingers that only trembled slightly, she unfastened the chain around her neck and slid off the wedding-ring that had hung there for seven years. She stared at

it for a long moment, then dropped it into her jewellery
box and shut the lid.

She could hear the mournful tones of the clarinet as
she walked up to the front door. There was no answer
to the bell, but it opened when she turned the handle
and so she let herself in. She hadn't come this far to be
turned away by something so slight.

The music was coming from the sitting-room, and
she made her way through, her heart in her mouth.
Her palms were damp, and she wiped them nervously
against the skirt of her dress—the silk jersey she had
bought for his party. Having made the decision, she
was going in with all guns blazing—but it took a lot of
courage.

She swallowed, and took the last few paces to the
top of the steps. Then she stopped and allowed her
starving eyes to absorb the sight of him.

He was standing with his back to her, one arm
resting on the window, his head propped against his
wrist, the other hand shoved into the pocket of the cut-
off shorts that were all he wore.

Her eyes travelled slowly over the breadth of his
shoulders, the smooth columns of muscle each side of
his spine that led the eye down to the narrow waist, the
sleek curve of his buttocks above strong, straight legs.
One knee was slightly bent, throwing his weight on to
the other, and in the fading daylight from the window
she could see the springy hair which misted his legs.

Despite her nervousness she smiled. He was beautiful, a generous, talented, warm-hearted man in his
prime—and she loved him.

Finally he turned, as if he sensed her presence, and his eyes were carefully blank.

'I didn't hear the doorbell.' His voice was harsh, slightly ragged. He crossed the room slowly to the stereo cabinet and turned down the music.

'I know. I hope you don't mind me coming in?'

He shook his head. 'Did you want something?'

She nodded. 'Yes.' You, she wanted to say, but she couldn't, not just like that, cold. 'I wanted to talk to you.'

A flicker of hope danced in his eyes, but he damped it down quickly. 'Do you mind if I get something on? I feel at a bit of a disadvantage. . .'

He walked towards her, and her eyes feasted on him, the slight sway of his hips, the ripple of muscle in his thighs, the broad expanse of his chest with its wild tangle of curls—she swallowed slightly, and he paused in front of her, his eyes searching hers.

'You look fine to me,' she whispered.

He groaned, a deep gust of sound from the bottom of his soul. 'Look, what's this all about?'

She took a deep breath. 'You said, when I was ready, you'd be here. You said you wanted all of me— my mind, my heart, my body. I'm not sure my mind's worth having, but it's yours, along with the rest, if you still want it. I only hope I'm not too late. The only thing is, I'm still not sure—I got the impression you wanted me to marry you. Am I right?'

He studied her in silence for a few endless seconds, and then a fleeting smile danced across his face.

'Only an impression? I must be losing my grip.'

'Well, you didn't really make it clear, and——'

'An oversight.' The corner of his mouth twitched into a smile, but his eyes were serious. 'Permit me to remedy it.' Taking her hands in his, he dropped to his knees in front of her.

'Ross, what are you playing at?' she said with a choked laugh.

His smile widened. 'I just don't want there to be any misunderstanding. Now, concentrate, please, Elizabeth—it is Elizabeth, isn't it?'

She nodded. His voice was still a little unsteady, and he was hanging on to her hands as if he was afraid she would run away.

'Good. Right. Elizabeth, over the last few weeks you've come to mean a great deal to me. It hasn't all been plain sailing. You crashed into my new car, threw me fully dressed into the pool, subjected me to countless indignities when I was unwell——'

'Ungrateful beast——'

'Don't interrupt, please! You make me lose my thread! Where was I?'

'Indignities!' she chuckled.

'Ah, yes. But somehow, through it all, you've managed to worm your way into my heart.' The smile died, replaced by a look of loving intensity that made her want to cry. 'I love you, Lizzi. I can't give you any guarantees, but as long as I'm able I'll do what I can to make you happy. I can offer you security, both financial and emotional. I'll never leave you, never be unfaithful to you, never hurt you deliberately or neglect your needs. I can't promise you fireworks, but for the rest of my life you'll have my friendship and companionship, and my undying love.'

He closed his eyes and swallowed, his throat working. Lizzi, unbearably moved, sank to her knees and rested her head against his chest.

'You still haven't asked me to marry you,' she teased gently, although her throat was clogged with tears.

'I'm afraid,' he whispered.

Lizzi was shocked. 'Afraid of what? I thought it was what you wanted?'

'You could say no——'

'Well, I won't,' she reassured him gently. 'I love you, Ross.'

His arms came round her and he crushed her against his heaving chest. 'I never thought I'd hear you say that,' he whispered brokenly. 'Oh, God, darling, I love you so much. . .'

She eased away from him and gave him a watery smile. 'You still haven't done it, have you?'

His brow creased in a frown, and then he chuckled weakly. 'Some people are never satisfied. Elizabeth, will you do me the honour of consenting to be my wife?'

'Yes,' she said promptly, and hugged him, then she stood up and pulled him to his feet, leading him up the steps towards the hall.

He trailed after her. 'Where are we going?'

'Bed,' she said airily. 'We've wasted enough time.'

He stopped in his tracks, and, as he weighed about five stone more than her, she stopped too, looking back at him with a puzzled expression on her face.

'What now?'

'We can't.'

'Why?'

He gave a short, frustrated laugh. 'Why? Are you on the Pill?' She shook her head. 'Anything else?' She shook her head again and tried to smile, but a terrible dread was forming in her heart.

'Would it really be such a tragedy if I became pregnant?' she asked softly. 'I mean, I'll understand if you don't want any more children, and I think the boys are great, but perhaps you think two's enough——'

His eyes blazed. 'You have no idea how much I want to give you my child—to watch your body blossom and grow, to see our children born and be there with you through the teething troubles and the hard times, not just the weekends and the holidays, but all of it, from start to finish. Tragedy?' He shook his head gently. 'It would be the greatest joy of my life. . .'

She went wordlessly into his arms, and his lips brushed hers with tantalising tenderness, teasing and tormenting before settling firmly against hers in a searing caress. He lifted her easily into his arms and carried her up the steps to the bedroom, laying her down carefully in the middle of the vast bed.

'Why this dress?' he murmured, his lips against the hollow of her throat.

'You said you wanted to take it off slowly and kiss every inch——'

'I remember,' he said with a smile. 'Promise you won't push me in the pool?'

She grinned impishly. 'Not for a while, anyway.'

'Minx.' His hand slid up her spine, found the zip and slid gently back down, then he eased the shoulders of the dress down inch by inch, trailing hot, moist kisses over her delicate skin.

When he reached the lace edge of the teddy, he groaned. 'Not this wicked thing again!' He worked the dress down to her hips and then eased it off the rest of the way, then peeled the teddy off with an agonising lack of haste, scattering kisses as he went.

Then she was naked, feeling intensely vulnerable. She tried to cover herself but he stopped her.

'No. Let me see you.' His face was taut, his lips slightly parted and his breathing ragged as he stood slowly and pulled off his shorts. As he looked down at her, his eyes were on fire. 'Oh, Lizzi,' he whispered, then he was lying full-length against her, his legs tangled with hers, their hearts pounding together, their lips clinging fiercely. Her nipples grazed against his chest, and she moaned, a desperate little sound that was torn from her throat. He caught it in his mouth, moving over her and lifting his head to lock his eyes with hers as their bodies meshed.

She cried his name, over and over, murmuring words of love and commitment as their bodies ebbed and flowed together. Then the tempo quickened and she was robbed of speech, making only wordless little cries to echo his as they hurtled together into oblivion.

As they settled gently back to earth again, she felt his chest shaking and she lifted her head away from him to study him intently.

'Are you laughing or crying?'

He chuckled deeply. 'I'm not entirely sure. My God, sweetheart, that was something else!' He closed his eyes and hugged her, then rolled to his side, taking her with him. 'Wow! I love you, Mrs Hamilton.'

'I'm not Mrs Hamilton yet!' she protested laughingly.

'Just practising.'

She traced his nose with her fingertip, down to his lip. He caught her finger between his teeth, growling softly, and she smiled, totally enchanted.

'Pussycat,' she murmured.

He growled again, and she laughed, startled.

'Tiger!' she said breathlessly.

With one swift movement he rolled her over and trapped her beneath him, his laughing eyes just above hers.

'Tell me you love me,' he commanded.

'I love you.'

'Again.'

'I love you. Do you suppose I'm pregnant yet?'

He smiled. 'Don't know. I shouldn't have thought so. What's the hurry?'

She lowered her lashes. 'Well, I don't know, you're getting terribly old, Ross, I don't think we should leave it too long—oh!'

Her eyes flew open again and she laughed breathlessly.

'How did you manage that?' she asked, smiling.

'I'll teach you to call me old!' he said, moving sinuously against her, and his lips came down and silenced her laughing reply.

Hours later they sat up in bed eating cheese sandwiches and drinking gallons of tea. They had slept and made love again, and slept again, only to wake ravenous.

'Mmm.' Ross slithered down the bed, stretching deliciously and grinning.

'You look like the cat that got the cream.'

'Uh-huh.' He grinned unrepentantly. 'You are some wild lady in bed, Mrs Hamilton.'

Lizzi blushed. 'It's you—you do all sorts of things to me I'd never dare to dream about, and I just fall apart.'

'Delightfully. Do you think you ought to ring your mother and tell her where you're spending the night?'

Lizzi chuckled. 'At two-thirty? I don't think she'll thank me, and, anyway, I imagine she has a pretty good idea. She had more faith in you than I did, I think.'

He turned on his side facing her, his head propped on his hand. 'Why did you come here tonight?'

'It was Edward—the clever man pointed out that, while I thought I was avoiding hurt by staying away from you, in reality I was already grieving for you because I already loved you. Nothing could be worse than last week.'

'Amen to that,' Ross murmured. 'I had a letter from the boys, going on about how wonderful you are and how much they hope we'll get married—I never did finish reading it. I couldn't get past the bit about you without howling my eyes out.'

She slid down the bed and wrapped her arms round him.

'I'm sorry,' she mumbled into his neck, 'I'll never leave you again.'

He hugged her close, and they drifted into a deep and dreamless sleep.

* * * *

In the morning he left at seven and went straight to the hospital in response to a call from Mitch.

When she got in at eight, there was a buzz of excitement on the ward. Lucy Hallett gave her a long, thoughtful look, and Mitch Baker positively avoided her.

Ross arrived at ten-fifteen with Oliver in tow, and collected her for coffee. She couldn't keep the smile off her face, and Ross didn't even try.

'Hi, precious,' he said softly, and kissed her cheek. 'Come on, we don't want to keep everybody waiting.'

'Everybody?'

He gave her an enigmatic and intriguing little smile. When they arrived in the coffee-lounge, a large group of people were standing laughing round the bulletin board. As soon as they were spotted, a huge cheer went up.

Lizzi looked up at Ross, a puzzled expression on her face.

He grinned, and led her forward. Like the Red Sea, they parted, and then she saw it; decorated in silver horseshoes and confetti, the cartoon showed her and Ross tobogganing down a wedding cake, Lizzi in a wedding dress, Ross in top hat and tails, and the caption read,

Ice Maiden Captured By Yeti! Cold War ends in icy alliance as the happy couple announce plans for marriage. The honeymoon will take place in the Himalayas, where the groom is reported to have a large family!

Lizzi gave a breathless little laugh. 'Tell me about your mother, Ross,' she said suspiciously.

He chuckled. 'Well, she's big and hairy and——'

Under cover of the laughter, he swept her up and into his arms and kissed her soundly, much to everyone's delighted approval.

'Sir?'

Ross lifted his head with a groan.

'With timing like that, Baker, you could get yourself struck off yet!'

Mitch scratched his head, embarrassed. 'Is it OK? It was a bit of a rush.'

Ross snorted. 'Just thank your lucky stars I didn't ring you at three in the morning to give you more time!'

'You were asleep at three this morning,' Lizzi said without thinking, and then blushed furiously.

Everybody laughed.

Well, nearly everybody. Mitch Baker wisely bit his tongue!

4 MEDICAL ROMANCES
AND 2 FREE GIFTS
From Mills & Boon

Capture all the excitement, intrigue and emotion of the busy medical world by accepting four FREE Medical Romances, plus a FREE cuddly teddy and special mystery gift. Then if you choose, go on to enjoy 4 more exciting Medical Romances every month! Send the coupon below at once to:

**MILLS & BOON READER SERVICE, FREEPOST
PO BOX 236, CROYDON, SURREY CR9 9EL.**

N O   S T A M P   R E Q U I R E D

YES! Please rush me my 4 Free Medical Romances and 2 Free Gifts! Please also reserve me a Reader Service Subscription. If I decide to subscribe, I can look forward to receiving 4 Medical Romances every month for just £6.40, delivered direct to my door. Post and packing is free, and there's a free Mills & Boon Newsletter. If I choose not to subscribe I shall write to you within 10 days - I can keep the books and gifts whatever I decide. I can cancel or suspend my subscription at any time. I am over 18.

EP19D

Name (Mr/Mrs/Ms) _____

Address _____

_____

_____ Postcode _____

Signature _____

The right is reserved to refuse an application and change the terms of this offer. Offer expires November 30th 1992. Readers in Southern Africa write to Book Services International Ltd, P.O. Box 41654, Craighall, Transvaal 2024. Other Overseas and Eire, send for details. You may be mailed with other offers from Mills & Boon and other reputable companies as a result of this application. If you would prefer not to share in this opportunity, please tick box. ☐

— *MEDICAL* ♥ *ROMANCE* —

The books for enjoyment this month are:

MORE THAN TIME Caroline Anderson
LOVING QUEST Frances Crowne
CLOSER TO A STRANGER Lilian Darcy
DIAMONDS FROM DR DALY Angela Devine

♥   ♥   ♥   ♥   ♥

Treats in store!

Watch next month for the following absorbing stories:

THE CALL OF LOVE Jenny Ashe
A HEART UNTAMED Judith Worthy
WAITING GAME Laura MacDonald
THE WESSEX SUMMER Sarah Franklin